Orphan Train Brides

Including

A Family For Merry

By

Caroline Clemmons

And

A Family For Polly

By

Jacquie Rogers

Table of Contents

PROLOGUE

These two novellas from the authors of *Mail Order Tangle* are expanded from previous inclusion in the *Under A Mulberry Moon* anthology.

Asked to help with recording who took which children from the orphan train, Merry and Polly Bird took advantage of the position. Determined to liberate five quirky, ragtag orphans not likely to be adopted by caring people, they vowed the children would not end up as they had fourteen years ago.

The rescue idea appeared to have merit—until the supervisor from the Children's Aid Society arrived. Single women were not allowed to adopt. Merry and Polly each had five days to find a suitable husband who wouldn't steal their share of the boarding house.

Become a bride or lose her children!

A Family For Merry

By

Caroline Clemmons

A FAMILY FOR MERRY

Chapter One

May 25, 1878, Mockingbird Flats, Texas

Merry Bird slid the cash box into the small safe. "Another week's rent successfully collected."

Her adopted sister Polly checked the ledger. "I'm relieved every month when our savings increase. You know I can't help myself, Merry. I always fear this will be the month we won't make our expenses and will have to dip into our savings to pay the butcher or the mercantile."

"We're doing well so quit worrying." Merry understood her adopted sister's misgivings were due to them having grown up as adoptees of terrible parents. Would her sister ever completely heal from their childhood? "Wouldn't those horrible Birds be surprised to see what we've accomplished?"

Merry examined her fingers. "I thought my hands were beyond recovering the right color and texture. Even four years later I recall the discomfort when they were broken out and bleeding."

Polly's expression sobered. "I'm surprised we survived. Certainly doing so wasn't because we had good care or decent clothes or comfortable places to sleep."

Merry hugged her sister's shoulders. "We're fine now and that's what counts. We have a great place to live, nice people renting from us, and people we can pay to cook and clean. I count us lucky in so many ways."

"You're right." Polly grimaced. "Well, mostly nice people. Mrs. Adams and Miss Cross can be a trial, can't they? That's beside the point."

Polly gestured around them. "I simply have to keep reminding myself this won't disappear."

"I wonder what the reason is for tomorrow's special committee meeting of the Women's Society? Vallie was mysterious when she came by."

Polly giggled. "Whatever her reason it must be serious to take time on a Sunday afternoon. I don't think the mighty Mayor Elton Collins appreciates looking after the children or having his day off from the bank disturbed."

Merry couldn't suppress her own chuckle. "My, my, he's far too important. You've only to ask him if you have any doubt."

Polly said, "I suspect he'll be off to Lucky's Tavern while Amaryllis keeps watch on her brothers playing in the garden."

From the dining room a gong called residents to supper.

Merry rolled her eyes. "I think Elvira takes out her frustrations by striking that gong."

"Better the disk than one of us."

Laughing together, the sisters walked into the dining room to help deliver food to their residents before they enjoyed their own meal.

***

Mockingbird Boardinghouse rent included breakfast and supper. For a small additional fee, a light dinner was available at noon. The exception to this was Sunday.

On Sundays, a large meal was served at half past one rather than in the evening. For supper, residents were offered crackers, cheese, and cornbread to eat with milk or coffee to drink while the cook took a half day off.

By half past two, Merry and Polly were on their way to the home of Vallie Collins for the Mockingbird Flats Women's Society meeting. When they arrived, several others were already there. Most stood near the refreshments displayed on the dining table even though no one appeared to be partaking of the desserts.

The local doctor's wife, Jessica Bushnell, smiled a welcome and patted beside her on the couch. "I'm glad you made it. Vallie went to tell the children in the back garden to quiet down."

Polly elbowed Merry and whispered. "Told you."

Ignoring her sister, Merry leaned toward Jessica. "Do you know why we're here?"

8

Jessica shook her head then looked toward Vallie, who'd returned to the room.

The mayor's wife glided in to pose by the piano. Her elegant coiffure and gown sent the message that she was an important person in this town. Privately, Merry thought the mayor and his wife were too impressed with his office.

"Ladies, thank you for coming. I'm excited to announce we've been given an important task. I'm sure you've seen the notices around town that an orphan train will be arriving on Wednesday at two o'clock. Our group has been selected to help, a wonderful honor."

Horrible memories ricocheted through Merry's mind and she reached for Polly's hand. They two of them had been so frightened when they'd been marched onto the train at barely age eight. Their worst fears were realized when Joe and Ruby Bird adopted them as well as choosing the boys, Bartholomew and Newton. The four children had lived in misery and fear for almost ten years until the horrid couple's death.

Vallie gestured to Sarah, the sweet-tempered preacher's wife. "Reverend Jones has volunteered the church for prospective parents to view the children. We're to keep records of which child is selected by whom. Ladies, I need at least six of you to volunteer."

Merry raised her free hand. After an elbow nudge and a squeeze of her fingers from Merry, Polly did the same.

Six other women also volunteered.

Vallie preened and wrote the names on her slate. "Merry and Polly, will you keep the records for us while the others shepherd the children?"

Merry looked at Polly before speaking. Even though Polly squeezed her hand hard and gave her a stern look, Merry smiled at Vallie. "We'll be pleased to do so."

On the way home, Merry was lost in thought.

"Why did you do that against my wishes?" Polly pinched her arm. "I wish you hadn't said we were going to see those poor children. Ever since I saw the notices go up in town I've been a bundle of nerves. You know some of them will go to awful homes like we did. I'm not sure I can stand watching."

9

Merry rubbed at the pinched spot. "I intend for us to see they only go to nice homes. Between us, we can make sure that, at least here in Mockingbird Flats, nobody like the Birds adopts children."

"And how do you think we can we do that?"

"I don't know yet, but we'll think of a way. We may have to wait until Wednesday at the church to figure out a plan."

Polly gave her an incredulous stare. "Mercedes Murphy Bird, you're planning deception inside the church?"

Merry raised her chin. "Whatever it takes, Polly. I won't be party to others going through what we endured, even if we did get our boardinghouse as a result."

Resentment tinged Polly's voice, "Hmph, those awful people could have lived for decades if they hadn't been so greedy. Then where would we have been when we turned eighteen? Out on our ears without decent clothes or money to live on, that's where."

Merry patted Polly's arm. "I know, I know, we've gone over this, dear. We're doing all right so let's be grateful for what we have."

Even though she advised her sister to display gratitude for their present situation, Merry couldn't stop the memories rushing to gnaw at her confidence and serenity. At least she'd had Polly to share with but theirs had been a hard and painful life. She was determined that any children they saw from the orphan train would not go to a home like they'd endured.

When they reached their wrought iron fence, Mary took pleasure in the neat appearance of their boardinghouse. Butter-yellow paint trimmed in white reminded her of sunshine. They'd recently had the sign repainted, *Mockingbird Flats Boardinghouse*, in white outlined with dark green lettering and border.

Mr. Nevins had painted a mockingbird on a branch under the name. The sight always boosted Merry's morale. Hanging below and attached by hooks was the smaller sign that announced *Vacancy*. Stored inside they had a matching one that said *No Vacancy*, which was the one they usually needed.

She and Polly found most of their residents gathered in the parlor. The sisters had arranged a small bookcase where residents could borrow books to read.

10

Gideon Warren, who was hard of hearing, took advantage of the books. He had often said, "I don't have to hear well to dwell in a book." He looked up and smiled before he returned to reading.

Their two widows, Flossie Adams and Letitia Fraser sat near the windows.

Mrs. Adams glanced up when they entered. "I don't suppose a poor widow could get a cup of coffee, could she?"

Merry smiled at the fussy woman. "Let me put my purse away and I'll get you one. Anyone else?" The few who looked up shook their head.

Letitia, or Lettie as she asked them to call her, continued her knitting. The friendly woman insisted her hobby helped keep her arthritic fingers limber.

Merry supposed they were fortunate they only had two complaining residents, Mrs. Adams and Miss Cross.

When she and Polly returned with fresh coffee, Lettie asked, "Have you heard when the new lawyer is coming? Poor Mr. Davis has been gone one month today."

Polly set a cup on the table beside Mrs. Adams. "He sent a wire that he'll arrive this week but we're not sure which day. His name isn't Davis though. He signed his wire as Blake Woolf."

Miss Cross looked up from her embroidery. "I suppose the sign will have to be repainted then. Is he going to live here?"

Merry admired the handkerchief Miss Cross was decorating. "He intends to use his late uncle's room. We left Mr. Davis' belongings there. Of course, we tidied as much as we could without being disrespectful."

Mr. Allsup, the telegrapher, looked up from his newspaper. "Davis was a fine man. His nephew has big shoes to fill."

Mrs. Adams set down her cup. "I for one am curious to see what this man looks like. What sort of last name is Wolf? I certainly hope he's not a red Indian."

With a sigh, Merry looked at the grumbling widow. "It's an English name spelled with two Os. W-o-o-l-f. His letter accompanying payment for us to hold his room and office was well written and professionally worded."

11

Which didn't prove anything, except that the man had been educated. They had such a nice family-like group in the boardinghouse currently. In spite of the fact that the boarders were older than her and Polly, Merry couldn't help feeling the mother to the group. She hoped this Mr. Woolf would blend in well.

Chapter Two

Blake Woolf stepped off the train and assessed the town of Mockingbird Flats. He wished he could have visited Uncle George while the man was alive. Getting away from home even now had been a problem but he'd finally managed. Not only had his great uncle left him his legal practice, he'd included a small legacy that helped Blake's mom—and made it possible for Blake to come here.

The stationmaster stopped in front of him. "I'm Michelson. You lost, son?"

He stuck out his hand. "Blake Woolf. Looking for the boardinghouse."

The man shook hands but summed him up and down before answering, "They know you're coming? Can't be sure of a room if they don't."

"They're expecting me."

Michelson nodded. "That's all right then. One block that way, west."

"Anyone who can deliver my trunk there?"

"Yancey Cameron will. Does odd jobs. I'll send him round with your gear."

"Thanks, I appreciate your help."

The man forked a thumb in a westerly direction. "Yep, you head thataway. Used to be a hotel. You can't miss it."

Blake wondered why people always added "you can't miss it" to directions when usually they were wrong. In spite of his misgivings, he hadn't gone far before he spotted the boardinghouse. Nice looking place, three stories high and looked to have been recently painted.

Pleasure shot through him when he spotted what would be his office on the front's east side, *Davis Law Office*. He'd have the name changed but not for a few months until after people got used to him. For now he would have his name added in smaller letters underneath

13

the present ones.

He strode up the walk and opened the front door. A room full of people stared at him. Wonderful aromas drifted toward him and reminded him he'd missed lunch.

One of the prettiest women he'd ever met hurried toward him. Her light brown hair was styled in a bun at the back but several locks had escaped to curl near her face. She was tall and willowy and moved gracefully.

Her pleasing smile and her sparkling dark blue eyes welcomed him. "You must be Mr. Woolf. I'm Merry Bird. My sister Polly and I are the boardinghouse owners."

He recognized her name from their correspondence but he was surprised at her age. She must be younger than he was. "Pleased to meet you, Miss Bird. You've saved my uncle's room?"

She reached behind a counter and handed him a set of keys. "It's number one at the top of the stairs on the right. Actually, it's over your office. If you'd like to go up, you have just enough time to put your bag in your room and refresh yourself before supper."

He climbed the stairs behind her, admiring the sway of her shapely hips. When he unlocked the door, the room was larger than he'd expected.

She stood in the hall but gestured inside. "You can see we left your uncle's belongings in the corner because we didn't know what to do with them. If there are items you wish to save, we have a small amount of storage in the attic and more over the carriage house."

"Thank you." Pretty as she was, he hoped she wasn't going to be intrusive.

She handed him a card that said *Welcome to Mockingbird Flats Boardinghouse* with some additional writing he hadn't had time to absorb.

"You'll see from this that breakfast is at seven, dinner at noon, and supper at six except on Sundays. I'll let you settle in while I go about my business. Welcome to Mockingbird Flats."

Before he could reply, she was disappearing down the stairs. He set his cases on the floor and poked into the armoire, chest of drawers, and washstand. An upholstered chair was in front of wide

14

windows. Beside it was a table with a large lamp.

He pressed on the bed and found the mattress satisfactory. As usual, he'd have to sleep at an angle to keep his feet from hanging over the bed's end. At least he wouldn't have to share this one. The quilt on top appeared new, the burgundy and green pieces cheerful and masculine.

The arrangement and size were luxurious after his family's crowded home. His uncle's belongings were stacked neatly in one corner. He'd go through those another day. For now, aromas of food had his stomach rumbling.

A small woman appeared carrying a large pitcher. Her frizzy hair was an almost startling shade of orangish-red. "You'll be wanting warm water for washing. Better hurry or you'll be late for your supper." She transferred water from the pitcher she carried to the one on his washstand.

"Thank you...." she was gone before he learned her name.

When he arrived in the dining room, he was met by a different smiling woman than the one who'd greeted him. This blond was equally attractive as Merry Bird but didn't create the same internal reaction in him.

"Mr. Woolf, I'm Polly Bird. Welcome to Mockingbird Flats Boardinghouse. Why don't you sit at this table? Your late uncle shared his meals with these three gentlemen. Bass Barnell is our deputy marshal, Gideon Warren is the barber whose shop is opposite yours at the front, and John Allsup is our telegrapher. In fact, John's the son of one of the very first telegraphers."

She spoke low, "Gideon's a little hard of hearing since serving in the war so please look at him when you speak so he can read your lips."

Blake took his seat. "Nice to meet you." Suddenly, he was tongue-tied. These men had known his uncle and he wondered what they thought of Uncle George and of him for not visiting.

At his right, Gideon met his gaze. The man looked to be in his fifties but already had gray hair. "Glad you're carrying on for George. Fine man and losing him was a tragedy."

Carefully he looked directly at the man. "Thank you. I was

fond of him and wish I could have visited."

Gideon waved a hand dismissively. "He explained about your mother needing you and what good care you took of her."

Relief relaxed his taut muscles. Perhaps these men wouldn't think him a poor nephew after all. He wanted their respect.

John looked to be in his mid forties, tall, and thin with smile lines on his face. His blue eyes twinkling, he pointed with his fork and chuckled. "Made you sound like a saint. You look like a regular person to me."

Blake grinned at the telegrapher. "Although I try to lead a good life, I'm hardly saintly. I'm sure any of my nine siblings will attest to that."

The deputy swallowed a huge bite. He was a tall, broad man with a long mustache that curled on the ends. "We can always use more who try to be good. Mostly that's what we have in town, but sometimes the rail line brings in drifters and troublemakers as well."

Blake set down his coffee. "Guess a lawyer wouldn't have much to do otherwise."

The woman who'd first greeted him swished by. "Everything all right here?"

When everyone nodded, she asked, "Is your room all right, Mr. Woolf?"

"Very nice and looks comfortable. I'll check the office after supper. I'll go through my uncle's things as I have time."

"Let Polly or me know if we can help." With a smile, she was off to another table.

He watched her then turned back to his food. "Odd arrangement for a boardinghouse. I thought residents always shared one big table."

Gideon waved his fork in a circle around them. "This was the dining room when this was a hotel. Merry and Polly changed it to a boardinghouse because they didn't think a hotel was proper for single women to operate. This way they can choose who stays here."

"Looks like you have music sometimes. Do professionals come in and perform?"

"No, when this was a hotel, they had dinner music on Friday

16

and Saturday evening. Now whoever wishes can play the piano."

"You lived here long?"

Gideon cut a bite of meat. "Since my wife died six years ago. So much easier since my shop is here. Of course, the railroad hadn't come in then. Didn't arrive until two years ago."

Blake asked, "Was there much traffic before then?"

John broke open his roll. "Not like now, but we had a fair share of cattle drovers, overflow from Fort Worth I reckon."

"Bet the previous owner is kicking himself for selling now that there's a rail line through Mockingbird Flats."

Gideon shook his head. "Could be, but I doubt it. He was getting older and wasn't in good health." He tapped his chest. "Bad ticker. Moved to California to live near his daughter and her family, enjoy his grandchildren."

Blake peered around the dining room. "Looks like a nice place. Uncle George wrote he liked living and working here. I didn't know if he was trying to ease Ma's mind or if he was truthful."

John cut a bite of his roast beef. "I have to say this is a much friendlier and nicer place to live now that the Bird sisters are owners."

Bass mopped his plate with the last of his bread. "That's true. Everything is kept nice and clean. For instance, they recently had the outside repainted. They spruced up inside first and we all appreciated that."

John chuckled. "A couple of the women will never admit it, of course. We're all friendly except for two of them." His gaze was directed at a table of three women.

The deputy leaned back in his chair. "There're always some who'd complain if they were hung with a new rope."

Blake smiled at the lawman. "My pa used to say 'If it was raining money some would complain about the small change' and I have to agree."

Gideon nodded. "Heeheehee. Now that's the truth. Reckon we ought to go on into the lobby, only now they call it the parlor."

Blake pushed back from the table and stood. "I believe I'll check out my office. I'm eager to get started to work. I need to find out how much business my uncle had."

Blake pulled his keys from his pocket and opened the door from the parlor into his office. Getting used to two entry doors would be an adjustment but he liked being able to go from the parlor into his office. He expected the two rooms to smell stuffy with disuse.

Instead, the scent of lemon and beeswax greeted him. All the surfaces gleamed with care. He doubted that was his uncle's doing, but had to be the result of the Bird sisters or their staff.

Tomorrow morning, he would make a tour of downtown, introducing himself to storeowners and businessmen. Hopefully, his business would consist of real estate purchases and wills. He couldn't depend on court cases since the courthouse was over ten miles away in Fort Worth.

Chapter Three

On Wednesday, Polly helped Merry organize their record keeping for the orphans. She and Polly were at the side of the altar where they could easily see the children and the prospective parents who'd come. A crisp tablecloth covered the table and draped almost to the floor in front. She and her sister sat on a bench provided for them.

Two matrons herded about two dozen children up the aisle and lined them across the altar as if they were going on the auction block. Tears burned the back of Merry's eyelids when she surveyed the children and listened to the matrons give orders. Painful memories stabbed her heart.

She glanced at Polly. From the grim expression on Polly's face, she must be experiencing similar memories. Although Polly had been at the orphanage longer than Merry, they hadn't actually met until they were put on the train.

Years of hard work in harsh conditions had Polly and Merry's hands broken out in bleeding sores before the couple that adopted them had died four years ago. She and Polly weren't blood kin, but they had been adopted together from the orphan train when they were both eight. Almost ten years of slaving for Ruby and Joe Bird had been hard.

The Birds decreed that if anyone ran away, those left would suffer for it. Out of loyalty to one another, Polly, the two boys, and she endured their servitude. She and Polly had managed to survive and then each had inherited a fourth of the mean-spirited couple's Nebraska estate.

The two boys adopted at the same time as them, Bartholomew and Newton, had each received a fourth of the inheritance. The young men went further west to homestead their own places adjoining one another. She and Polly hadn't lived in the same place because the boys

slept in the hay loft while the girls slept in the home's attic space—
both places freezing in winter and hot in summer.

A flood of recollections rushed at her and threatened to carry
Merry into despair. She fought to reclaim her normally optimistic
outlook. She had so much to be grateful for now. Focus on the good.

Reverend Zebediah Jones stood at the church door, as if to bar
anyone he thought unfit. Merry had confidence the kindly preacher
would do just that. Too bad no kindly minister had protected her and
Polly—although the Birds put on a good act in front of others.

Some children wore hopeful expressions, some fearful, some
so downtrodden their eyes were those of old people in young faces,
and others looked only at their feet. Several particularly tugged at
Merry's heartstrings—the ragtags, the unadoptable. What would
happen to them?

Couples from town came forward and chose one or two
children. Of course Fiona and Brent Bushnell would be good to the
boy they adopted. Gwen and Marshal Nate Canup also adopted a boy.
Lavinia and Dennis Zimmerman chose a girl of four who Lavinia
carried as they left.

Helga and Gustav Swenson had lost their sons to diphtheria last
year and chose two brothers. Sophie and Dieter Mayer had lost two
children in the same epidemic and selected a girl and two boys. Sophie
cried with happiness as they ushered their new children away.

Merry recorded each couple's names and the names and
identification numbers of the children they selected. She was
comfortable, believing these children would receive good treatment.

A scrawny little girl whose nametag said *Abigail* wore a
pinafore too large that drooped off one shoulder and had a torn pocket.
Her hair looked as if she wore a bird's nest. The poor child limped
badly, but something was off there.

Merry whispered to Polly, "Notice she changes legs for her
limp."

Abigail hovered around a toddler labeled *Tamara*.
Occasionally, Abigail brushed against Tamara and the baby would cry.

Polly leaned toward Merry. "Did you see Abigail pinch the baby? I think she wants her to appear disagreeable so they can stay together."

Merry gazed at the two girls. "Tamara is a pitiful sight. Her nose needs wiping. Do you suppose she's old enough to blow her nose?"

Polly pretended to pick something up from the floor in front of the table. "The baby has red spots everywhere on her exposed skin."

Merry stood and walked around the table. On closer inspection, the spots appeared to be from a paint crayon. Sorrow and mirth warred inside Merry.

What an ingenious child Abigail was. The poor girl must be frantic thinking she'd be parted from Tamara. Merry wondered if they were sisters.

A boy whose nametag said *Calvin* stood with feet braced, arms crossed, and a mulish expression locked on his face. His age would be around nine, a very desirable age for a boy. He glared as if he dared anyone to adopt him. No one did.

Merry got Abigail's attention. "You must be tired from standing on your injured leg while taking care of baby Tamara. Why don't you both sit beside me?"

Abigail pulled at a lock of her disheveled hair. "Both of us? You mean Tammie can stay with me?"

Merry smiled as reassuringly as she could. "Yes, that's what I mean."

Abigail picked up Tammie and deposited her at Merry's feet then promptly sat beside her so that she and Tammie were obscured by the tablecloth's skirt.

Merry motioned to the boy. "Calvin, I can see you don't need anyone to look after you, but would you help me by standing beside Abigail to make sure no one bothers her or Tammie?"

He didn't move for a full minute before he inhaled and released a deep breath. "S'pose I can." Slowly, he ambled to stand behind Abigail and Tammie, as if daring anyone to touch the girls.

Merry wrote the names of the three children on the list and her name as the person adopting. To mask the fact there was no husband, she wrote her first name and then sort of scribbled her middle and last name in what she hoped passed for a husband's name. Murphy Bird could be a man's name, couldn't it?

Beside Merry, Polly whispered, "What have you done?"

"You know exactly what I've done. I am not deserting these children to chance."

Polly's eyes sparked fire. "Neither am I."

When the matron nudged a boy labeled *Noah* forward, she announced that he was mute but followed directions. He clutched the hand of a girl whose nametag said *Evelyn* and who appeared younger than him. The little girl was thin except for swollen joints and belly. She leaned on Noah as if she could hardly stand.

Polly stood. "You can put my name down for Evelyn and Noah. You know that no one will adopt a boy who's mute, at least not for any decent purpose, and clearly that little girl is ill."

Polly rose and stepped over to the two she'd chosen. "Evelyn, Noah, I'd like you to come live with me."

Noah stood clasping the girl's hand, his brown eyes holding suspicion. After a brief exchange which the girl translated, hope sprang into the girl's eyes as she clung to Noah's hand.

"I'm called Evie. Noah don't never talk. He's good to watch out for me and he's real smart."

"I'm sure he is. He won't have to talk at our house unless he wants to." Polly took Evie's free hand and led the two to the table.

The children sat on the floor beside Polly's chair. They chose the same spots as Abigail and Tammie at the table's other end. When Polly had reclaimed her place, she leaned near Merry. "Can we really get away with this?"

"Proceed as if everything is secure and above board. We can't let these children suffer as we did just because we don't have husbands. We can do this, Polly. Both matrons are busy talking to Vallie and Jessica."

Merry wasn't as familiar with the other rural families but she'd heard nothing bad about them. Reverend Jones had welcomed each couple. Hilde and Arvid Larsen had a dairy farm and selected the two oldest boys. Lena and Jurgen Webber wanted strong boys, but had

22

shied away from the belligerent look on Calvin's face and the fact that Noah was mute. Instead they chose two slightly younger boys. Claudia and Steven Bailey chose a girl and a boy.

Elsa and Martin Witt, local ranchers, chose a girl and a boy. Ingrid and Espen Olsen also chose a girl and a boy. Maybelle and Orville Darnell had come to adopt only one boy but accepted two since they were the only children remaining.

From where the matrons stood, probably only Calvin was visible. "Calvin, perhaps you'd like to rest by sitting down behind Abigail.

With his gaze focused on the matrons, Calvin dropped to the floor and sat with his legs crossed and his elbows on his knees. The clever boy understood the need to disappear.

Merry checked her lapel watch. "Ten minutes until time for the matrons to head to the train and depart for Fort Worth."

Merry stood, carefully avoiding stepping on a child, and took the list to the matrons.

After appearing surprised there were no children remaining, the senior woman in charge beamed at Merry. "All the children gone to good homes, isn't that wonderful? Thank you, ladies, for your help."

Vallie and Jessica escorted the matrons toward the train. The other volunteers also left.

Reverend Jones walked beside Merry to the table she and Polly had used. "I suppose you think I didn't notice you each acquired a family of your own?"

Merry smiled at the kindly minister. "You also know they'll each have a wonderful home with us. We'll love them as if we'd given birth to them."

"If I didn't believe that was true, I would have alerted those two matrons who appeared more interested in talking than in doing their job. To be kind, I suppose traveling with only children leaves them starved for adult conversation."

Polly held her children's hands. "We have room, plenty of wholesome food, and a good place for them to live and grow." She spoke to the children. "Aren't you excited?"

Merry picked up Tammie. "Let's go to your new home,

children. You'll love living there."

The sisters hurried toward the boardinghouse by a route that avoided the matrons. No point in calling attention to the fact no men accompanied them.

Chapter Four

In the boardinghouse, Merry and her sister took their new families to their suite at the back of the first floor. She and Polly had separate bedrooms and there was a vacant bedroom between them. Their place had seemed spacious but with five more they would be snug.

Polly stood with hands on her hips. "I'm moving to the vacant suite on the third floor. It has two sleeping rooms so everyone will be less crowded."

Merry hadn't been without Polly for fourteen years. Already she sensed a loss, as if part of her had been ripped away. Looking at the situation logically, she realized Polly's decision was the right one.

"We've been together so long, Polly, I'll be sad to see you leave this suite. I understand why you want to move, though. If you'd prefer, I can move up there."

"You have three and I have two children, so my moving makes more sense. Besides, Noah is quiet so he and Evie won't disturb anyone."

Evie's face clouded as if she was about to cry. "You're not gonna keep us?"

Polly hugged both children to her. "Of course I'm keeping you. I mean we can move upstairs so we have more room. Come on, I'll show you how nice it is. You can see all over town from the windows." After exchanging a meaningful gaze with Merry, she took Evie's hand and led the two toward the stairs.

"Calvin, I'll show you to your room." Merry opened the door to what was currently Polly's room. "We can decorate it to look more masculine."

He stood barely inside the room and stared. "You mean nobody else is sleeping in here?"

"Just you. The girls will be next door and then I'm next. Will you be a… all right in here alone?" She'd almost asked if he'd be afraid, but caught herself.

He narrowed his eyes. "And nobody else's stuff will be here?"

"As soon as my sister moves her things upstairs only your things will be in here. I'll only come in to clean and to tuck you in at night. I won't bother your things if they're put away."

He scowled. "Don't have nothing to bother."

"You will have. We'll go to the mercantile tomorrow and get you new clothes, toys, and books."

Except for crossing his arms, he appeared ready to run. "What do I hafta do to keep them?"

"Just be yourself, Calvin." She crossed her heart with her forefinger. "Honest, I give you my word this isn't a trick. This is your new home. I'm your new mother and I will love and protect you with all my might."

He stepped inside the room and sat on the bed tentatively as if afraid it would suddenly swallow him.

"Come on, Abigail and Tammie, so I can show you your room."

Merry noticed Abigail's limp had miraculously disappeared.

"You're in the middle between Calvin and me. For now, you'll have to share a big bed, but I'll get Tammie a smaller one of her own soon."

"I don't care if she sleeps with me. Are you gonna be my new mother too and love and 'tect me?"

"I certainly am. You and Tammie and Calvin are my children now and this is our home. If you need something, you should tell me."

Abigail tugged on Merry's skirt. "I needa pee."

Merry pulled the chamber pot from under the bed. "This is for you to use unless I'm available to take you to the privy out back."

She looked at Abigail. "Does Tammie know how to use the chamber pot?"

"Mostly she does but sometimes she forgets. You're not going to spank her when she has an accident, are you?"

"Of course not." This was a part of adoption Merry hadn't considered thoroughly. In fact, acquiring three children was a spur-of-

26

the-moment decision. She had no idea how to potty train a toddler but she didn't regret taking charge of Tammie with her other two.

She knelt down. "Tammie, this is for you to go potty, all right?"

Tammie pushed a finger inside her mouth and stared at Merry then at Abigail.

Merry hated to resort to bribery, but this was totally unfamiliar territory. "You know, good little girls get treats here."

"Did you hear that, Tammie? We can be good, can't we?" Abigail finished her business and straightened her clothes. "Come on, I'll help you."

The toddler let Abigail assist her while Merry observed the little girl handle the toddler as if she'd done so many times.

"Did you often help Tammie?"

"Matron 'signed me to her. Bigger kids always helped small ones."

Merry nodded. "Yes, I remember. You see, my sister and I were in the orphanage and then on the orphan train, too."

Abigail's eyes grew round. "You were? Did you get a nice Mama?"

She shook her head. "Unfortunately, the people who adopted us were mean. I want to be a good mother and see you and Tammie and Calvin are loved and have good food and a safe place to live and lots of time to play."

She would, too. Not for a minute did she regret her deception with the adoption records.

"Let's see what you have with you, shall we?" She opened the tiny bag each girl was given. All she found inside was a nightgown and a change of clothes. "Don't you have a doll or stuffed animal?"

"No, we had to leave them for the children who didn't go on the train. Tammie cried for her little lamb. I didn't cry but I wanted to bring my dolly."

"Tomorrow, we'll go to the mercantile and buy you new clothes and shoes as well as books and a new dolly and toys. Maybe they'll even have a stuffed lamb."

Polly returned to the suite. Noah and Evie were with her.

Gideon and Bass followed, each carrying an empty box.

Quickly, Polly packed clothes into her trunk. "We came to carry my belongings upstairs. Gideon and Bass volunteered to help me move."

Merry said, "I can help, too."

Polly shook her head. "Get your children settled." She closed the trunk's lid.

Bass hefted the case. "We've got this covered, Miss Merry."

Polly filled a box with knick knacks and her toiletries. Gideon carried that and headed for the stairs. She emptied drawers into the other crate. She loaded Noah's arms with loose items.

Bass returned and took charge of the second box. "Anything else?"

Polly scanned the room then took a picture from the wall. "That's it, I think. If I forgot anything, Merry, you know where I'll be." She laughed and left the suite.

Merry sank onto a chair. She was happy to have the children with her but not having Polly share the suite created a strange hole in her heart. They'd been together so long she sensed the void immediately.

Abigail and Calvin and Tammie stared at her.

Calvin asked, "Are you sorry you got us?"

His question snapped her from her reverie. "No, I'm really pleased to have you. Why would you think otherwise?"

"You sure looked sad. Figured you were gonna send us back."

Merry motioned with both hands. "Come here, all three of you."

She sat Tammie on her lap and hugged Abigail to her side. She doubted Calvin would appreciate a hug so she took his hand. "I'm so glad you're my children. I'm never, ever sending you back to the orphanage. The only reason I'm a little sad is that my sister moved to another part of the house, but it's all right. She's still here and I'll see her every day."

The gong's peal echoed through the house and Tammie grabbed Merry around the neck.

Abigail also clung to Merry. "What was that?"

"Don't be alarmed. That was Mrs. Elvira Koch, who is our cook, banging our gong. When you hear that sound, you know your meal is ready. I'll bet you're hungry. Let's go to the dining room and have our supper."

Merry took the children to each table and introduced them to the residents. Calvin didn't greet anyone, but stood scowling at each group. Abigail spoke shyly and Tammie clung to Merry's skirts.

At the men's table, Gideon shook hands with Abigail and Tammie. Calvin kept his hands in his pockets.

Undaunted, Gideon smiled. "Nice to have you here, children. Young faces brighten up the place. You're lucky to have Miss Merry as your new mother."

John Allsup dabbed at his mouth before speaking, "Yes, you are. She'll take care you're always provided with the best, same as she does for us."

Blake Woolf, the new resident, sent her a guarded look. "Adopted without being married? Must be new rules."

She sensed herself blush. "I don't need to be married to love and protect these children, Mr. Woolf." She shepherded her charges. "Come, children, our table is just over here."

She and Polly had always eaten together, but Merry chose a table previously unused and settled Tammie on a chair. Drat, the child needed a high chair. She was considering what to do as a temporary measure when the lawyer appeared beside her.

"I have just the thing. I'll be right back." He headed toward his office and soon returned with two thick books he stacked on the chair. "These should do the trick."

She studied him. He was the handsomest man she'd ever met. His dark hair waved slightly and was cut short. He must be at least six feet tall if not an inch or two over that.

"Thank you. I thought you didn't approve of the children."

He met her gaze with such directness her knees wobbled. "I have nothing against your children. My question was strictly about whether or not you followed the law."

As if he didn't know very well she hadn't. Her voice probably sounded sharp when she said, "Thank you for your assistance."

29

He nodded and returned to his seat.

Dora Farris appeared with plates balanced on her arms. "Here you go, you darlin's. Eat up."

Calvin didn't need encouragement and attacked his food as if afraid it would be stolen unless he hurried. Merry didn't chide him because she remembered having to eat quickly. He'd slow down on his own once he realized no one would take his meal from him.

Abigail ate almost as rapidly but glanced to insure Tammie had enough. Merry helped Tammie by cutting her meat and vegetables into bite-sized pieces. The toddler used her hands instead of fork or spoon.

More memories shoved into Merry's consciousness. The orphanage, the train, the scarcity of food at the Nebraska farm—even though the Birds had plenty for themselves. She pushed aside those recollections lest they steal the joy from having her own children in her own pleasant home.

Chapter Five

Blake couldn't keep his gaze from straying to Miss Merry and her three recently adopted—illegally—orphans. The children's manners were atrocious yet she didn't reprimand them. Miss Polly's two were the same, but apparently he couldn't prevent directing his focus toward Miss Merry.

Something about her mesmerized him. She was beautiful and graceful but so was her sister, Miss Polly. But, Miss Merry was the one who captured his attention and inspired daydreams.

Gideon nodded toward the object of his attention. "Miss Merry will give those children a fine home. Much better than she and Miss Polly had, that's for sure."

That grabbed Blake's attention. "You mean they were orphans?"

John set down his cup. "Adopted by a miserly couple who used them like slaves." He chuckled. "Only they came out winners in the end. Couple had officially adopted them, see. When the Bird couple died from their own greed, Miss Merry and Miss Polly and two boys inherited the estate. That's how they could buy this hotel."

Blake didn't quite get the whole picture. "I don't understand what happened?"

John leaned forward. "The couple bought two rhubarb pies and brought them home but they didn't let the children eat a bite. Mr. Bird ate an entire pie and then went to bed. His wife ate about three-quarters of one and followed him. Next morning, he was dead and she was out her head. One of the boys went for the doctor but the woman died before the doc arrived."

Bass pointed his fork at Blake. "The children—who were really teens by then—would no doubt have been blamed. The woman who baked the pies contacted the preacher to find out who bought her pies. She was young and didn't know the rhubarb leaves are poisonous and had let them simmer with the rhubarb. Her family had been sick, too, but they'd only had one slice each."

John dug into his scalloped potatoes. "Yessirree, the Birds' greed was lucky for Miss Merry and Miss Polly."

Bass reached for another roll. "Lucky for us, too, 'cause they sure improved our lot in life. Easy to understand why Miss Polly and Miss Merry wanted to save those children."

Blake pondered the new information. He knew many adoptees were mistreated, but there were supposed to be safety procedures. Evidently that process had failed the Bird sisters.

That was neither here nor there. The last thing he wanted was to be around a bunch of children. "Saw a couple of small boys on the stairs. Any other children here?"

Gideon gestured to the table where the two small boys sat with two adults. "Those are the Randall boys, Sammie and Austin, with their parents, Eunice and Sam. Good boys for the most part. Sam works at the mercantile and they're living here until they can afford to buy a house."

Blake nodded. "Ah, well, I didn't mean the boys had disturbed me. You can't expect young children to be quiet all the time, can you?" He couldn't afford to make a bad impression. Besides, he knew firsthand how young children behaved.

Bass reached for yet another roll, the last in the basket. "That's why the Bird sisters had Yancey Cameron put up a couple of swings in the back yard. Lots of space to run back there, too."

"He's the man who delivered my trunk from the station. You know, I haven't looked around the property. Been concerned with my uncle's belongings and his practice."

John sent him a sympathetic glance. "Understandable. Terrible about George dying so young but I'm glad he had you to take over for him."

Blake probed for information from the other men at the table. "From what I've gathered, he did a lot of real estate transactions."

Bass used a bite of roll and sopped up the last smear of gravy from his plate. "He sure did. Knew people all over the area, too. 'Course he also did wills and such. Say, you could handle the

32

children's adoptions for the Bird sisters."

Although he didn't respond he sure as heck thought no, thank you. He wasn't about to get tangled up with the Bird sisters and their orphans. Sure, he could understand their motives. That didn't excuse them breaking the law.

Currently, he figured he had all the lawbreaking he could handle.

***

The next morning, Merry and Polly took their children shopping. Christmas morning couldn't have been better than treating these dears to new clothes and a few toys.

Calvin was clearly perplexed. "You mean I get to keep this stuff just for me? I don't have to give it to anybody?"

Merry laid a hand on Calvin shoulder. He stiffened she quickly removed it. "These things belong just to you, Calvin, and not to anyone else. You can invite other boys to play with the toys if you want to but you don't have to."

Calvin held his treasures close. "Don't know any others 'cept Noah. He has his own now."

Merry arranged to have their purchases delivered this afternoon.

Polly rubbed her hands together. "Why don't we all go to the confectionary store for a treat?"

Merry took Tammie's hand. The toddler was getting tired of shopping but had been good so far.

Outside, they met Mr. Woolf. "This looks like a fun outing."

Abigail tugged at his hand. "Know what? We got new clothes and I got a dolly. It's nicer than the one I had at the orph'nage. Tammie got a bear because they didn't have a lamb. I got new shoes, two pair so I can save one for church. Do you go to church too?"

He smiled as if he'd understood her rambling. "Yes, I'll be going to church. Where are you headed now?"

"We're going to get a treat from someplace called the con… con…" she looked at Merry for help.

"Bea's Confectionerary a couple of doors down."

Abigail tugged on his hand again. "Why don't you come with

us? Do you like treats?"

He looked poleaxed but recovered. "I think I will. I'm making the rounds to introduce myself to business owners and I haven't met Bea yet."

Merry couldn't have been more surprised. "You need not feel obligated because Abigail invited you. We understand you're a busy man."

He sent her an inscrutable glance. "I always have time for a treat with a beautiful woman."

She exchanged gazes with Polly, who appeared as shocked as Merry. "Children, remember the rules. If you want to come back another time, you have to be on your best behavior."

They crowded into the small shop. In addition to stools at the counter, there were three tables, each with four chairs.

Bea Quentin, shop owner of Bea's Confectionery, smoothed her apron. "What a lovely group. What can I get for you today?"

Blake stepped to the counter. "We'll have sarsaparillas and cupcakes all around."

Abby clapped her hands. "Did you hear, Tammie? We get sar'prilla and a cupcake."

Polly protested, "Mr. Woolf, surely you don't intend to treat all of us."

"My pleasure, ladies and gentlemen." He paid Bea and then gave a slight bow. After he delivered two of the drinks he went back to the counter for more.

Merry sat and pulled Tammie onto her lap. Abigail and Calvin joined her. Polly and her two sat at the next table.

When Bea and Mr. Woolf had delivered all of the drinks and cupcakes, he sat at the table beside Calvin. "You don't mind if I sit beside you do you, Calvin? We men have to stick together."

Calvin sat up a little taller and almost smiled. "Yeah, we men have to stick together 'cause we're outnumbered."

Mr. Woolf saluted Noah with his glass. "Isn't that right, Noah?"

Noah grinned and raised his drink as Mr. Woolf had done. Although Noah still hadn't spoken, seeing him smile was heartwarming.

The lawyer carried on a conversation with the children but sent her glances that left her puzzled. He was usually gruff yet he was quite kind to the children. She simply couldn't figure out Blake Woolf.

They were having a lovely time when Evie suddenly threw up. The poor child was horrified and embarrassed. Bea rushed over with towels and she and Polly wiped up the mess.

Big tears rolled down Evie's cheeks. "I'm sorry. I couldn't help it. Does this mean I can't ever come back?"

"Don't worry, dear. Of course we'll come back." Polly pulled her onto her lap and hugged the little girl.

Bea returned with a clean wet towel to wipe Evie's face. Polly rocked the child and cuddled her.

Mr. Woolf stood and bent over Polly and Evie. "Why don't I carry her back to the boardinghouse for you? She probably needs to lie down."

Polly was almost in tears. "Thank you, Mr. Woolf. She has so much trouble with her digestion."

After gently picking up the little girl, Mr. Woolf cradled her in his arms. "Don't worry, Evie. I'm sure your mama will soon have you feeling fit."

Merry made certain they hadn't left anything behind then herded her children toward home.

***

Blake strode toward the boardinghouse. He had no idea what had come over him to accompany the Bird sisters and their illegal adoptees. As it turned out, he was glad he had so he could carry the poor little girl home.

He had no business spending money as if he had deep pockets. While he rebuilt his uncle's business he had to watch every penny. Although, he was finding discrepancies in Uncle George's records that alarmed him.

He couldn't decide if Uncle George was careless, an inept attorney, or receiving payback for deliberate errors. He truly hoped it wasn't the latter. He'd always looked up to Uncle George and hoped his faith wasn't misplaced.

35

From what he had found so far, his uncle handled a lot of real estate deals. If those deals were contested, Blake would have to bear the fallout. How could he defend his uncle's position?

In thinking over the problem, surely Uncle George would have had more money if he'd been dishonest. His mother would be broken-hearted to learn otherwise so he would proceed as if Uncle George made honest mistakes.

Please, God, let that be the case.

Chapter Six

For over a week since she'd brought them home, Merry searched for a way to break down the wall Calvin had erected around himself. She understood he didn't trust adults after the life he'd led, but she wanted him to feel safe and cared for. So far, he wouldn't talk about his life before she adopted him.

Nothing she'd tried had made a dent in Calvin's armor. When she spotted him go into the lawyer's office, she was about to tell Calvin he shouldn't pester Mr. Woolf. Curiosity kept her silent.

Although she'd told the children not to bother the other residents and to never, ever go in Mr. Woolf's office or the barber's shop unless she was with them, she was surprised Calvin had set foot in the law office.

Calvin stood at one side in his usual stance with feet braced and arms crossed. His position allowed her to see his face as well as that of the lawyer. "How come you don't like children?"

Seated at his desk facing the door, the lawyer's face revealed his surprise. "What makes you think I don't? Didn't I buy you sarsaparilla and a cupcake the other day?"

"Most of the time, though, when you look at us your face gets that mean look." Calvin narrowed his eyes and scowled. "See, like that."

The boy's frank appraisal made her smile. At the same time, her motherly instincts were on alert in case the man was unkind to her son. If he did anything to hurt Calvin now that the boy was finally adjusting to being in a family, she would show Blake Woolf the sharp side of her tongue.

Instead, the attorney appeared to be struggling to keep from smiling. Even from this distance mischief shone from his eyes. "You know I have to defend nice people against mean ones, right? Reckon I have to practice looking hardhearted so when I go into court I can scare the cruel people. We can't let them win if we can prevent that, can we?"

Calvin uncrossed his arms and stuffed his hands into his pockets. "Mean people should never win."

The boy's face fell. "Sometimes they do anyway."

Woolf laid aside a sheaf of papers he'd probably been reading before Calvin interrupted him. "That's true, but I always do my best to see the good people win. Unfortunately, sometimes the judge appoints me to defend a mean person, someone I'm sure is guilty. Know what I do then?"

Calvin almost smiled. "You don't do a good job."

The attorney shook his head slowly. "Wrong. I still do my very best. See, sometimes it appears a person is guilty when they're not. The law says every person is innocent until proven guilty and that everyone deserves a fair trial."

"But what if they were caught doing the crime? Or, what if they admitted to you they did it?"

"If I know for certain they committed an offense, I try to talk the person into pleading guilty in private, but in court I do the best I can to prove them innocent."

Calvin shook his head. "But, that's not right. Guilty people should go to jail. If they killed someone like a man did my pa, they should hang."

Merry's breath caught in her throat.

Mr. Woolf stared at Calvin a few seconds before he answered, as if he were choosing his words carefully. "You know what an oath is, right?"

"Cussin' like…," he leaned forward, "Bad words I ain't allowed to say no more cause Mama'll wash my mouth out with soap for sure if I say another one."

Merry almost gave herself away by laughing.

Mr. Woolf shook his head. "That's one kind but not in this case. An oath is like a promise you can never break. Ever. When I became a lawyer, I took an oath on the Bible to defend each person I represent to the best of my ability. A real man never goes back on his word."

Calvin sat on the floor beside the lawyer's desk, a thoughtful look on his face. "So if you knew I murdered someone but I said I didn't and you were my lawyer, you'd have to try to get me to go free?"

"That's correct. I'd have to look for ways to prove you were innocent. That's called the defense. Now the person representing the court would be looking for proof you were guilty. That's called the prosecution."

"I'm asking you now to be my lawyer." Calvin stood and put coins on Mr. Woolf's desk. "When I grow up, I'm gonna find the man what killed my pa and I'm gonna kill him."

Merry clutched her throat. Poor Calvin.

Mr. Woolf gestured for the boy to come closer. "Calvin, let me tell you why that's not a good idea. You're nine, right? So, maybe for the next ten or eleven years you'll be thinking about this man."

"That's right. I ain't never gonna forget him or that I want him dead as my pa." Calvin's voice sounded fiercer than his years.

"In your insides those thoughts will be churning and festering worse than a sore that won't heal. You know who that will hurt? Not the man who killed your pa." He pointed at Calvin. "You'll be the one damaged by your hate."

Calvin stood and rested his hands on the end of the desk. "You sayin' I should let him get away with killin' my pa?"

"I know that sounds hard but that kind of person never just does one thing wrong. Eventually he'll get caught. You don't have to do anything unless you know he's on trial somewhere. Then, you could go and tell the prosecution that the man is guilty of killing your father, but you'd have to have proof. Do you?"

Calvin swiped his eyes on his sleeve. "I seen him. I was eight, but I seen it happen. He woulda killed me, too, but I run away and hid. I took care not to be anywhere he might notice me. That's how come one day them Children's Aid people picked me up and put me in the orph'nage. 'Fore I could run away I got put on that train what brought me here."

Merry had tears in her eyes as well. Finally she knew Calvin's problem. She wanted to rush to him and cuddle him in her arms but she knew he would never allow that. She remained still and continued eavesdropping.

Mr. Woolf said, "That must have been frightening. You're very brave to act so fast and get away."

"Y-You think so? I been worried I shoulda stayed and helped my pa."

The attorney shook his head. "You couldn't have helped him if you were killed too. Are you certain your father died?"

"Yeah, he'd yelled before the man stabbed him and a neighbor come running. I hid and watched but I knew he was dead from the way he fell and all the blood on him."

"That was quick thinking. How did you live after that?"

Calvin shrugged. "Lots of children live on the streets and alleys, mostly boys but some girls too. Some—I ain't saying I did— but some mighta learned to pick pockets and pick up stuff a body left lying around."

The lawyer nodded instead of passing judgment. "Sounds like a hard life but I meant what did you eat?"

"Mostly what we could find from rubbish bins behind cafés and stuff. You'd be surprised what people throw away."

"I guess I would. My family didn't throw anything away unless we gave it to the hogs."

"You mean you were poor? You dress real nice and have a big office and all so I figured you had lots of money."

Mr. Woolf shook his head. "I'm the oldest of ten children. My mother wasn't well, mostly from having too many children. If I wasn't helping my father, I was looking after my brothers and sisters and my mother."

Calvin nodded sagely. "I reckon that's why you stay away from us now. You probably seen all the children you want."

The lawyer laughed. "Something like that I guess. Don't tell a soul, but I don't dislike children, I just don't want to be in charge of them right now."

"Not even when you get married? Aren't you going to have your own children?"

40

Blake Woolf leaned back. "Whoa, son, slow down. I'm trying to breathe life back into my late uncle's law business. I can't afford to marry yet. So far, I can't even afford to buy a house."

Calvin stretched out his arms. "But, you don't need to, you live in ours."

Merry stepped from the shadows and called to her son, "Calvin, have you forgotten you're not to bother Mr. Woolf?"

Calvin resumed his defensive stance. "I had to ask him something."

The lawyer stood when she entered his office. "We were discussing the law. He hired me and paid me a retainer. I am now officially his lawyer." He picked up the five pennies Calvin had placed on the desk.

"If your business has concluded, Calvin, you should leave Mr. Woolf's office."

Calvin grimaced and stuck his hands in his pockets. "Yes, Mama." He ambled slowly toward the suite in which they lived.

When Calvin had gone into the living quarters, she turned to the lawyer. "Thank you for being kind to Calvin, Mr. Woolf. I've warned the children not to come to your office."

"Why do you call the other men at my table by their given names and not me?"

Stammering, she refused to meet his gaze. "Well… I've… known them almost four years and we… we only recently met."

"Nice try, but I don't think so. In the future, please call me Blake."

"I'll try to remember. In the meantime, I'll let you get back to work." She hurried out of his office.

How could she admit his presence sent her heart fluttering and directed her thoughts toward things she had no business thinking? Not just because he was the most attractive man she'd ever met, either. There was something about his manner that inspired trust and confidence.

Oh, she was being silly as a schoolgirl.

Chapter Seven

Blake reread his mother's letter.

Dear Son,

I hope this finds you well. Don't worry about me for I am fine. I have good neighbors who check on me regularly. Preacher Farris comes by twice a week.

I might as well start with the news that will disturb you and get it over with. Jessie has run off and married Hector Evans and they're living with his parents. You remember where they live, don't you, the farm between here and Marshall? I know they're old enough but they're both young for their age—especially Jessie acts several years younger than eighteen. I think they'll be all right with Hector's parents to guide them. I remember it's a good farm.

In the same week, we learned Lily's husband is being transferred to San Antonio. It's a grand promotion and I'm proud for them. With their three children they're awfully crowded where they are. They think the move and rise in salary will allow them to find a house with more room.

I've heard from Ella and she's expecting her third in five months. They're happy as can be even though they're bursting at the seams of their little house there in Longview.

I haven't heard from Gene or Marvin again since they got to California. I hope they've found the gold they were prospecting. I imagine the one who's really making the gold is the one selling supplies, don't you? Ha ha!

Mable still likes living up in Idaho. Sounds real pretty there in summer but I wouldn't like it in winter. Too cold for me but she says she doesn't mind and their two boys like the snow. They've learned to ski and have sleds.

Son, I suppose you'll be upset to learn about your youngest brother's decision. A couple of days after you left Vernon concluded Jefferson didn't offer enough opportunities. When he had a chance to work on a ranch down near the coast, a real big one, he took it. I've just had just the one letter but in it he said he likes the work. From the way he mentioned someone named Sally several times in his letter I expect him to wed soon.

Oletha is still living with her in-laws. I can't see them moving out on their own as Billy will inherit the farm from his parents. She's expecting her second this fall. She gets along real well with Billy's parents so that's a piece of good fortune.

Marlene is hoping to visit soon, bless her heart, or so she always says. She hasn't been able to get away since they bought that store in Austin. Just the two of them running the place makes it hard. Hopefully they can hire help soon. Their oldest, Tom, is seven now and helps out some with sweeping up. Little Amy just turned five but Marlene said Amy tries to dust the shelves. Someday the children will be a lot of help.

I am so proud you are set up in a nice place, son. George was partial to you and I admit I am too. You've always been so good to me, especially since your pa passed on. I hope you are meeting new friends and that one of them turns out to be a nice girl you can settle down with and have a family of your own. You deserve the very best.

Write soon. All My Love,
Ma

He would like to wring the neck of several of his siblings. The selfish pigs didn't give a fig about their mother's care. She'd been frail since the youngest was born eighteen years ago. Ten babies in ten years were too many too close together.

He paced back and forth wondering how he could insure his mother was all right while he took care of business here. He didn't see any way except to go to Jefferson and check on her. What could he do when he got there?

The gong sounded. Worry had chased his appetite but routine sent him to the dining room and supper.

Gideon peered at him. "You look all het up about something?"

He took his seat and pulled his napkin across his lap. "Sorry, didn't know it showed. Had a letter from my mother."

John asked, "Not bad news I hope?"

"Afraid so. My two sisters who are supposed to be checking on her aren't and my younger brother left as well. One sister's moving to San Antonio and the other has married and is living with her in-laws several miles away. Kid brother went to South Texas. Don't know quite what I'll do but I have to do something."

"Why don't you bring her here?" Merry set his plate in front of him.

He hadn't realized his landlady was standing there. "I-I hadn't considered that. Not sure how she'd do with two flights of stairs."

"We could help her up and down. You could check on her daily. Do you think she'd enjoy our company?"

Of course she would. She'd have to be crazy not to enjoy this place after the tiny room she was in now or the dilapidated house she'd lived in before that.

He let the idea sink in. "I imagine so. She's easy to get along with and not a demanding sort."

Merry laughed and laid a hand on his arm. "In that case, you should definitely consider moving her here."

He met her gaze. "Is there a room available?"

"There is. Could the sister who's living with her in-laws bring her here?"

"I'll arrange for someone to do so." He leaned back in his chair. "Whew! I feel better already." He dug into his food with renewed appetite.

After a few bites he realized someone was missing. "Where's Bass?"

Merry drifted by again, refilling coffee cups. "He had to take evening duty for someone who was sick. Dora is taking him a basket."

John chuckled. "He does like his vittles. Reckon he'll be glad to see her."

After Merry had joined her children, John tapped Blake's arm. "You give thought to bringing your mother here. After hearing about her from George, I feel as if I know her."

44

Gideon pointed at him. "She'll be welcomed and you'll be able to quit wondering how she's doing. You know she'll like the food."

"She'll enjoy everything about this place, with the exception of the extra stairs. Still, I'll be right here if she needs anything."

John set down his coffee cup. "We'll all help. We're like a big family here. We take care of one another."

He leaned back in his chair, struck by the truth of John's statement. "This *is* like a family. I'm lucky George left me his practice. I thought I had Ma set up safe and secure in Jefferson but I was wrong. I'll be glad to get her installed here."

Chapter Eight

Blake was writing up the will for a client when Calvin came to the door. "You need something?"

"Mama said I can't come in there and bother you but I need to ask you a question."

He laid aside his pen. "Go ahead and ask."

"I seen you watching Mama and I know you think she's pretty."

Drat! Blake didn't realize he'd been obvious. "She and Miss Polly are both pretty. Don't you agree?"

"Sure, but Mama's prettiest. I figured since you think she's pretty you could ask her to marry you. Then we'd be a real family."

"You're already a real family, son. I appreciate the invitation, but that's not how marriage works. I'm sure your mother wants to marry for love. She could have been wed long before now otherwise."

"She's real lovable. You could love her if you tried. I figure she'd fall for you. I seen her watching you, too."

Whoa, that was news.

"Calvin, you're a fine boy but you can't arrange marriage for other people. You have to let nature take its course. Miss Merry would be upset if she knew you were talking to me like this."

"It'd be worth a whippin' to have you and her get hitched. I know you wouldn't hit her or get drunk and spend all the money on drink and gamblin'."

"You know Miss Merry won't whip you. You're correct in the other, though. I've never hit a woman in my life and I don't get drunk or gamble. But, lots of men treat their wives with respect."

Calvin grimaced. "Pffft. And lots don't."

"I want you to talk to me whenever you have a problem, but right now I have to get this client's will written and delivered to him.

46

He's very sick and for it to be valid, he has to sign the papers. I don't want to take a chance he'll die before he's signed his will." He picked up his pen and dipped it into his inkwell.

Calvin looked at his shoes. "Okay, but think about what I said. Please?"

"I will." That didn't mean he'd act on Calvin's plan.

Calvin turned and ambled toward the suite where he lived.

Blake shook his head. So, Merry had been watching him, too, had she? How about that?

He would have to be more careful about letting his mind and his attention wander her way. If a nine-year-old noticed, then adults were sure to pick up the same way. If he were going to marry now, he wouldn't mind hitching up with Merry Bird.

But he wasn't. Not for several years when he was making enough money to support a wife. For now, getting his mother here was probably all he could handle.

After he returned from delivering the will, Blake wrote letters to Jessie and Lily and asked them to help get Ma moved here. Then, he wrote Ma.

Dear Ma,

How would you like to live here in the boardinghouse with me? I have arranged a room for you and have asked Jessie and Lily to get you moved here. Jessie especially could come with you. I told her I would pay her and Hector's train fare both ways if they helped you move to Mockingbird Flats. Guess it could be like a honeymoon trip for them.

I've already told you what a pleasant place this is to live. I haven't seen any of the rooms except mine, but that one is comfortable and large. The food is the best you'll ever eat—not to say anything against your cooking, mind you. They have a cook and a couple of helpers, though, so I imagine together they have an easier time than you ever did.

The owners are Merry and Polly Bird. I thought they were sisters but they are both orphans who were adopted from the orphan train together. I don't know how old they are but younger than me.

47

People of all ages live here, but most are around your age. Everyone is really pleasant except for two. One older widow named Mrs. Adams gripes a lot but I think she just wants attention. A young spinster named Miss Cross lives up to her name by not being cheerful. Even they are not too off-putting—or maybe I've gotten used to them. Ha ha!

Send me a telegram to let me know when you'll arrive. I've enclosed enough for your ticket and for Jessie and Hector and for expenses.

Your loving son,
Blake

He figured his flighty baby sister would jump at the chance for a free trip. His meager savings were disappearing faster than he'd planned. Maybe Ma had held on to some of her money he'd given her from Uncle George's inheritance.

Chapter Nine

As she dusted the parlor, Merry caught Blake sitting at his desk with a painful look on his face. "Are you ill?"

He jumped. "In a way." He motioned her inside his office. "Could you come in and close the door?"

Puzzled, she set aside her cleaning supplies and went into his office to sit in front of his desk.

"How well did you know my uncle?" He shook his head. "I don't mean that the way it sounded. I mean, do you think you knew him well enough to be a judge of his character?"

"Well… I suppose. He was a very nice man. I don't think he'd felt well for some time before he died. None of us picked up on anything specific. After he died, though, several of us admitted we'd noticed little things."

"Such as?"

"I'd noticed he was slower. He walked slower on the stairs and occasionally stumbled on a step. He ate slower at mealtime and sometimes had trouble swallowing but I credited that as him getting older. Actually, I thought he was many years more than the fifty-three he actually was."

"Anyone else comment?"

"John said he didn't laugh as much. Gideon thought his skin wasn't as healthy in appearance. Mrs. Adams said she'd known he was ill for several years before he died but that he wouldn't take her advice and see the doctor. I don't know if that's hindsight or not. Why?"

"I'm finding a lot of… well, discrepancies in his work. I wanted to know if he was careless or crooked or ill." He pinched the bridge of his nose. "Have to tell you I couldn't face him being crooked."

She laid a hand on the desk. "Oh, Blake, I'm sure he was honest. As far as I know he was a sweet man who should have gone to the doctor. In fact, perhaps he did and didn't let anyone know. Why don't you check with Doctor Bushnell?"

The lawyer leaned back in his chair. "Reckon I will. I've always looked up to Uncle George and he's the reason I became a lawyer."

She stood. "I'm glad I could set your mind at ease."

***

Blake slipped from the boardinghouse to find the doctor's office. He knew doctor's kept their patient's details in confidence just as a lawyer did. Since his uncle had passed away, there was no reason to keep his health a secret.

He recollected seeing the doctor's sign a few days ago and went into the office.

The doctor was seated at his desk perusing what appeared to be patient files. "Mr. Woolf, what ails you?"

"Nothing personally, but I need your help. That is, if my uncle George Davis consulted you in the months before he died."

The doctor's expression became a blank, his eyes hooded. "Why would you want to know?"

Blake held up a hand. "I know you keep patient's treatment and ailments secret, but this is important. Frankly, I'm finding discrepancies in my uncle's records. I couldn't bear learning he was crooked. Miss Merry Bird suggested I speak to you."

Dr. Bushnell chuckled. "Oh, she did, did she? Sounds like something she'd do." He indicated a chair near his desk. "I don't think George would mind me revealing at this point that he did come to see me. He was scared and he had reason to be."

A weight slammed into Blake. "In one way I'm relieved but I'm sorry for Uncle George. What was wrong with him?"

"He was losing control of his muscles, including his eyesight. He had a fairly new ailment you may not have heard of yet. If I hadn't been reading a medical journal about the disease the evening before George consulted me, I might not have been able to identify his problem so quickly. I'd never before diagnosed it in anyone."

Blake repeated, "What was wrong?"

"He had Amyotropic Lateral Sclerosis. It was discovered in

50

1869 by Jean Moutin Charcot." Dr. Bushnell leaned forward. "There is no cure. George was fortunate to have a heart attack when he did. Otherwise, he would have had a slow, terrible death."

His poor uncle. Conflicting thoughts warred in Blake's mind. His mother, his siblings, his future children—were they at risk?

"Is this… amyowhatever inherited?"

"No, so you and your family are safe." Dr. Bushnell pulled a piece of paper toward him and wrote on it. "Here's the name. Don't dwell on it, Mr. Woolf. You were special to George and you've done exactly what he wanted. I believe he had a happy life here made happier knowing you were caring for his sister and would take over his practice."

"Thank you, doctor. I can't tell you how much you've relieved my mind." He stood and made his way slowly back to the boardinghouse. What a burden his uncle carried and how like him not to worry anyone else by sharing his terrible news.

Blake wasn't ashamed of the moisture pooling in his eyes. He admired his uncle even more than before. Gazing upward, he renewed his vow to honor his uncle by being the best lawyer possible.

***

Merry carried the post to the parlor and handed out mail. Most residents rarely received mail, which is why they lived in the boardinghouse instead of with or near relatives. She motioned her sister to follow her to her suite.

Merry waved a postcard. "Look, Polly, a message from Bart."

Polly took it and shook her head. "What can they be thinking? Going up to Idaho to look for silver and abandoning their homesteads in Colorado, they must be mad."

Merry patted her sister's shoulder. "They're young and fit and have no cares or responsibilities. I'm glad that at least they're traveling together. As for me, I prefer being here in our lovely boardinghouse."

Polly huffed. "Did you see the last line? 'No, Polly, we haven't lost our money—all safely in the bank.' They think they're so clever."

Merry chuckled. "They are if they've traveled around for nearly four years without spending their inheritance. I'm relieved they still have their nest egg. After all, they could have gone wild and

51

gambled it away…" Unable to continue, Merry stopped and stared at the envelope she held.

"What's the matter?" Polly peered at the return address. "Oh, no. Open it quickly."

Merry ripped the seal and pulled out a single sheet of paper. Staggering to the closest chair, she thought she might actually swoon for the first time in her life. "No, no, it can't be. Oh, Polly, he's coming here. Reverend Grover Ecclestone from the Children's Aid Society is arriving in two days."

She turned to her sister. "Thank goodness the children are playing outside and didn't witness me reading this. What will we do?"

Tears shone in Polly's eyes. "We're in trouble. I'm *not* giving up Evie and Noah, I can tell you that."

Merry crumpled the letter with her clammy hand. "And I refuse to relinquish my three children. We'll simply have to make Mr. Ecclestone see how well off the children are with us."

"They're happy here. You know Evie wouldn't get the medical care she needs back at the orphanage. Noah is beginning to relax and trust me. I won't let some misguided do-gooder steal them."

"I'm going to consult our lawyer. He should know what we can do to retaliate." Merry sailed from her private suite with her sister following. She knocked on Blake's doorframe. Unless he had a client, he kept the door open to the parlor. She closed it behind her and Polly.

Blake stood. "May I help you, ladies?" He gestured to two of the three chairs near his desk.

Merry smoothed out the crumpled letter and handed it to the lawyer. "We won't let him take our children and need you to tell us what other choices we have."

He appeared to study the letter for a few moments before he looked up. "This is perfectly clear. You must each be married in order to keep the orphans. Does either of you have a prospective groom?"

Merry looked at her sister then at Blake. "Not that we've considered. We know that if we marry, we lose all control of the boardinghouse and our bank accounts. There are those who would love to obtain both without the work that went into getting here."

He looked from her to her sister. "Sadly, you're correct that in

52

Texas the husband owns all the property in a marriage and that includes your bank accounts. I must warn you that he could then dispossess you without you having any recourse, even though it is now and should remain your boardinghouse."

Merry's frustration mounted and she fought to keep from screaming.

He held up a hand. "Don't get angry with me. I know it's an unfair law, but I had nothing to do with passing it. However, I'm bound to uphold it."

Polly leaned forward. "There must be something we can do that's legal and doesn't mean losing the children or the boardinghouse."

"I wish I could help you, but you'll have to get yourselves out of this mess unless you have prospective grooms to wed before this man arrives. You knew you were breaking the law when you brought those children here. I understand why you wanted them and your motives are noble, but misplaced."

Merry's anger dissolved into panic. There had to be a way to keep the children and their home. "I suppose you would have left them to their fate."

He leaned forward and rested his forearms on his desk. "Hard to say since I wasn't put in that position."

Merry snatched back the letter. "Thank you. Let us know what we owe you." She stood and rushed from the office to her suite before she burst into tears.

***

Blake watched the sisters hurry from his office and across the parlor. Even though Polly had moved upstairs, they both fled to Merry's suite. Through his doorway they'd left open, the inquisitive stares of several residents swiveled from him to the owners' suite door the sisters had closed behind them, and then back to him. What did anyone believe he could he do?

He resumed reading through his uncle's papers. Tried and failed. He was sorry he'd ever talked to the children. Once he had, they ceased being names and became people.

He remembered how light the little girl Evie was. She was way

53

too thin and Polly had taken her to the doctor. He hadn't heard what the diagnosis was yet.

Calvin made him chuckle at the same time his heart ached for the kid. Imagine an eight-year-old seeing his father murdered in front of him and having to hide to keep from becoming the next victim. Blake should have asked him if he knew why the killer stabbed his dad.

Each of the kids was precious. Not wanting to be saddled with children yet didn't mean he didn't like them. No, these five unusual specimens were good and deserved to remain here.

He shoved his paperwork aside and locked his street door then stepped into the parlor and locked the door behind him.

"Quitting early, Mr. Woolf?" Lettie's fingers moved the knitting needles in the red yarn as if motorized.

"Thought I'd take a stroll around the grounds. Would you like to come with me?"

"Not today, but thank you. I want to finish this sweater for the little girl who's so thin. Don't think I'm playing favorites as I intend to make one for each of the children."

"I understand. I'm sure they'll each appreciate your kindness." He dipped a nod and strolled out the back door.

The back yard was a crowd of children. Except for Noah, each one must be trying to yell loudest. He recognized the five the sisters had illegally adopted, the two Randall boys, and the preacher's children.

Two swings were in use and children also climbed trees. He watched, hoping no one fell. One of the trees would be great for a tree house.

What the heck was he thinking? He turned and was about to stomp back into the house when a tiny hand grabbed his.

Abigail held Tammie with one hand and him with her other. "Thank you for buying us a sar'prilla and cupcake, Mr. Woolf. I never had sar'prilla before."

"You're welcome, Abigail. Do people ever call you Abbie?"

"Sometimes. Mama calls me Abigail."

"You know…" he started to say she shouldn't count on Merry

54

being her mama but caught himself. That wasn't his place and he didn't want anyone shooting the messenger.

"Do I know what?" She stared up at him with such trusting blue eyes he felt like a rat.

"You take really good care of Tammie."

A bright smile crossed her small face. "She's my sister for real now that Mama brought us here. You know Mama and her sister are 'dopted too?"

"That's what I heard. Mama's sister is your Aunt Polly." No, he shouldn't encourage the deception. Before he could talk his way out of that—or into more trouble, Calvin sauntered over.

"They botherin' you, Mr. Woolf?"

"Not at all. I came out here to see where you play. Looks like a nice yard with lots of big trees."

"Yeah, we need more swings. We aren't allowed to go to the creek unless Mama is with us. She's scared we might drown. I like climbing the trees. Did you climb trees when you were a boy?"

They needed to learn to swim. There must be a place deep enough on the creek. Dadburn, there he went again.

"When I could. I had a lot of chores that took up most of my time when I wasn't in school."

"Even in summer?"

"Especially then because that's when a farm is busiest. We had planting and chopping weeds and watering and harvesting vegetables and putting by food for us and the animals."

"Whew, I'm glad I don't live on a farm. I like it here, don't you?"

That took him aback. "Yes, I do. I always hoped I'd get to move into town one day. Now I have." He didn't hate living on the farm, but this was better by far. If only his ma was here where he could check on her.

The back door opened and Merry and Polly came out on the porch.

Merry called, "Children, time to get washed up for supper."

Polly said, "Mary Elizabeth, Abraham, your parents will be expecting you. Come back tomorrow and play some more."

55

The minister's children raced toward home while the Randall children and the five new illegal adoptees went inside.

Merry snapped, "You, too, Blake Woolf. We don't hold supper for lollygaggers."

Man, she had a sharp tongue when she wished. He'd thought before she was well-named for she smiled whenever he'd seen her. Today he'd witnessed a different side of the lovely lady.

Chapter Ten

The next day, Blake sat sifting through more of his uncle's papers.

Calvin came in and laid a nickel on the desk. "I want to hire you."

Blake met the boy's gaze. "You've already hired me, remember. I'm officially your lawyer."

Calvin shook his head. "This is for something else. Miss Merry was crying last night so I peeked. She was worrying over this paper. After she went to bed, I read it. That man from the orph'nage is coming to try to take us back."

Blake wouldn't lie to the boy. "I'm afraid that's what he intends."

"Well, you got to do something to stop him taking us."

The hopeful expression on the boy's face cut right into Blake's heart. In this instance he wished he had a magic wand to help the children.

"The law is clear, Calvin. Only couples were supposed to adopt."

Calvin leaned on the desk. "If you married Mama, then you two would be a couple and we wouldn't have to leave. Them Mama would quit cryin' and worryin' and we'd be a real family."

"Calvin, I told you that you can't arrange a marriage for other people."

This old-man-in-a-child's-body gave him a knowing stare. "I asked around. If you're a grownup, you can. So why can't I?"

"One, you're not a grownup. Two, Miss Merry doesn't know you're talking to me. Three, I'll ask the woman I marry without help from a third party."

"Will you ask the male head of her family for her hand?"

"Well, sure I…" Too late he realized he'd stepped right into

57

Calvin's trap. "Ah, no, no, no, I see what you're doing. You're a clever boy, but you are not the head of her family."

"She said I'm the man of the family and that makes me the head. So, I'm givin' you my permission to court Mama and ask her to marry you and save us."

Blake shook his head at the boy's determination. If he ever had a son, he hoped he'd be as strong and brave as Calvin. The child's eyes shone with pain and loss that ripped at Blake's insides.

Merry came to the door. "Calvin, we talked about this. You can't bother Mr. Woolf."

Calvin leaned toward him and spoke quietly. "Will you at least think about what I said?"

Blake nodded. "I will consider the possibilities. No promises."

Calvin actually offered a small smile.

Walls closed in on Blake. He leaned back and shut his eyes. What could he do to help Merry and Polly?

Dadburnit, he couldn't even decide what was he going to do about his uncle's blunders?

***

At supper, John Allsup brought Blake a telegram. "Came this afternoon. Wasn't anything you needed to take care of immediately."

"Thank you, John." He wasn't quite sure about the protocol of offering a tip to the telegrapher as you would a delivery boy. While he pondered that, he opened the wire.

"Hope you don't mind if I read this at the table. Reckon it's from my mother."

Arriving Friday three o'clock stop Jessie and Hector also stop

John chuckled. "She isn't paying extra for explanations is she?"

Blake folded the paper and put it in his pocket. "She's scrimped so long she does so automatically."

John nodded and pulled his napkin across his lap. "Said all she needed to, didn't she?"

Gideon asked, "Merry and Polly have a room for her?"

58

Polly appeared at his shoulder. "We do. We haven't figured out where we'll put your sister and brother-in-law, but we will."

Blake picked up his fork. "Anyone have a sofa in their room?"

Gideon nodded. "None of the men. Might borrow a cot from somewhere."

"Won't be for long so I guess I could sleep on a pallet in my office. Then my sister and her new husband can use my room."

Merry stopped. "We have a cot in the attic."

Blake liked that idea. "I could set that up in my office. Where will you put the… other guest?"

Her lovely face clouded. "I'd like to put him in the creek but I suppose that won't do."

"You have a second cot?"

"Yes, we do. Where do you propose we set up the thing?"

"I could share my office. Not a way to win him over, though."

Gideon asked, "Who's this that you don't like who'll be staying here."

She spat out, "Mr. Ecclestone from the Children's Aid Society. He's coming to check on the orphans who were adopted."

Bass said, "You can put someone in my room and I'll bunk at the jail for a few nights."

Merry paused with the coffee pot in her hand. "I couldn't ask you to do that."

"Knock off a few cents from my rent then. I like it here and appreciate all you've done to make the place nice for us."

She offered an almost-smile. "I'll give you a free month's rent if you let this man from the Children's Aid Society stay in your room for a few days that might turn into a week."

Bass leaned back and asked, "Done. He coming to make trouble for you and Miss Polly?"

"He's going to try." Her face puckered and she waved her free hand. "Excuse me." She turned and hurried into the kitchen.

Bass slapped his forehead. "Durn, now I upset her."

Blake shook his head. "She was already plenty upset. Has been since that letter arrived yesterday. The rules clearly say that a couple has to adopt."

59

John set down his coffee cup. "You know the legal system. Can't you find a way for the sisters to keep those kids?"

"Not unless they marry right away." Blake dug into his food.

When he looked up, all three men at the table stared him.

He raised both his hands in protest, hoping they didn't take the gesture as surrender. "Hey, I'm not a bigamist and not itching to wed."

Gideon leaned forward. "You couldn't do better than one of those sisters."

Bass nodded and pointed his fork at Blake. "I've seen you watching Miss Merry so I reckon you wouldn't be too miserable putting your shoes under her bed."

John pointed his finger at Blake. "You going to let this man from the Children's Aid Society ruin the lives of these good sisters and their five children?"

"Why are you picking on me? You're as eligible as I am."

Blake hated being pressured. Between his mother's welfare and his uncle's mess of documents, he figured he had enough on his plate.

John shook his head. "Isn't the same. You're the right age."

"There's no *right* age. The rules don't say the parents have to be a certain age, just that there are two of them."

He pointed his fork at Bass. "You're not that much older than I am. Why haven't you stepped up and asked one of the sisters to marry you?"

Bass' face turned bright red and he leaned forward. "Here's the thing. I'm sort of married."

Blake stared at the man. "How can you be 'sort of' married?"

The deputy exhaled with a whoosh then leaned back in his chair and crossed his arms. "You see, Neva Jo went home to her parents five years ago. She never got a divorce so reckon I'm still married. Leastways I send her part of my salary every month."

Gideon frowned at Bass. "Man, all this time you never said a word about a wife. You tried making up with her?"

A mulish expression settled on the deputy's face. "Naw, if she wants to go off and live with her parents then let her. I'm sure not begging any woman to stay with me."

Bass unfolded his arms and waved. "That's not the point here.

We're trying to help Miss Merry and Miss Polly."

Merry stopped at the table, her eyes red but no longer crying. "Help us do what? If you're talking about the rooms, we have that worked out now that Bass is letting us use his room for a few days."

Bass swallowed so hard his Adam's apple bounced. "That's good, Miss Merry. I'm moving my things to the jail first thing in the morning. You just say the word if there's anything else we can do."

"Thank you, gentlemen." Merry turned toward the table where her three illegal adoptees waited. Not before Blake noticed her red eyes were accompanied by dark circles underneath.

He drained the last drop of coffee from his cup and returned it to its saucer. "If you'll excuse me, I have sorting through my uncle's things waiting for me." He pushed back from the table and escaped to his office.

Chapter Eleven

The following day, Merry inspected Bass' room carefully. Sue Travis, a resident who worked half days for part of her rent, and Dora Farris, their full time employee, had changed linens and cleaned the deputy's room first thing this morning. She and Polly weren't taking a chance that this would be the time the efficient women overlooked something.

Polly stepped inside. "Sorry, but I had to clean up Evie's pancake eruption. Poor child. I'm so nervous I may dissolve into tears any moment."

Merry checked the water pitcher and then the chamber pot. "I hardly slept at all last night."

"Me either. And Evie being sick this morning at breakfast didn't help. I don't know what to do for her. She's so sweet and being sick embarrasses her as well as keeping her feeling bad."

Merry sympathized with Polly and with Evie. "The weak tea and crackers don't help settle her stomach?"

"Not at all. Honestly, sometimes I can actually see the muscles of her stomach knotting and cramping. And the stuff that she excretes. Honestly, I've never seen or smelled anything like it."

"Poor little dear. I'm sure you'll discover a way to help her. At least now she and Noah know her being sick won't cause her to be punished."

Polly's shoulders sagged as she sighed. "Well, this looks better than he probably deserves so let's go. He's due in a few minutes."

Snakes roiling in her stomach, Merry followed her sister down the hall. She had reviewed the eligible men who'd courted her. Unfortunately, she still didn't think of one she would trust with her children or her boardinghouse—or, for that matter, with her person.

Polly stopped at the end of the hall at the head of the stairs. "Evie's lying down so I'm going to go check on her. Noah's with her,

62

of course."

"I'll let you know when that man arrives."

Merry continued to the parlor where she picked up Tammie. She couldn't stop pacing while Abigail watched.

Blake came out of his office. "Perhaps you'd like to use my office for your meeting with this man, um," he paused and looked at Abigail, "you're expecting."

"Could we?" She set Tammie on the floor. "Abigail, would you take Tammie to your room and let her take a nap? Be sure she uses the potty first."

Abigail took the toddler's hand. "Come on and I'll show you a book."

Before Merry realized what she'd done, she'd grabbed his arm, her voice low. "You mean we can have our confrontation in your office, don't you? I don't intend to let my children go without a fight. I've never had a hissy fit, but one may be called for."

He patted her hand where it rested on his arm. "Then I'll act as referee. I must say you're always smiling and proper. I can't imagine you having a 'hissy fit' as you call it."

He grinned. "Mind you, as an older brother to six sisters I've seen some major of such encounters."

She looked at the older man who had just entered. "Prepare yourself for one of volcanic proportions."

She strode to meet him. "Mr. Grover Ecclestone?"

The smiling man set down his valise but retained his grip on a briefcase. He was of medium height with gray hair, a small beard, and wore spectacles. "Correct. Are you one of the owners of the establishment?"

"Merry Murphy Bird. My sister is upstairs. You'll be in room four on the second floor. Do you prefer to refresh yourself or meet with us first?" She handed him his key.

He pursed his lips before answering, "Perhaps we should get down to business now."

She flagged down Sue. "Would you tell my sister that we have a guest? On your way, perhaps you could set Mr. Ecclestone's bag in Mr. Barnell's room."

She turned back to their unwelcome guest. "We include breakfast at seven and supper at half past six. Cook rings the gong at those mealtimes. If you wish the noon meal, there's an extra charge."

The man gave the parlor a measuring gaze. "Very pleasant place. I'm surprised a boardinghouse is so large."

"This was built as a hotel with a nice assortment of rooms and suites until my sister and I converted it four years ago. All our rooms are occupied at the present. Bass Barnell, our deputy marshal, has moved to the jail to allow you use of his room while you're here. Otherwise, the only rooms for rent are in Lucky's Tavern or a boardinghouse across town. We've changed the linens in Mr. Barnell's room, of course, but ask that you allow him the privacy of not prying into his personal effects."

The lawyer continued peering around. "My, my, that's generous of the deputy. Of course, I'll be respectful toward his things. I can't imagine a tavern being as suitable or inviting and I do want to be on this side of town."

Mrs. Adams and Lettie watched from their favorite chairs in the parlor's corner. Eunice Randall sat nearby pretending to read a magazine while her boys sat on the floor with their toys.

"The deputy's being compensated for his generosity. Now, perhaps you'd like to follow me where we can conduct our interview in private."

She strode toward Blake's office as Polly hurried down the stairs, looking as if she were going to the guillotine. Merry shared that feeling. Mr. Ecclestone looked to be a pleasant man but Merry harbored a poor opinion of any man who would try to take her children and Polly's.

Blake closed the door behind Polly and went around his desk. He extended his hand to the man from the orphanage. "I'm Blake Woolf, the ladies' attorney. Won't you have a seat?"

Mr. Ecclestone shook hands with Blake then chose the seat at the lawyer's right.

Merry and her sister chose the other two chairs.

Blake gestured to the minister. "I suggest we hear from you first."

64

Ecclestone pulled documents from his briefcase. "It's come to my attention that neither of you ladies is married, yet you claimed orphans from the train. That is against policy, as I'm sure you know. I'll have to remove the children and take them with me."

Merry crossed her arms. "You *cannot* take our children. They're now feeling loved and wanted and are blossoming. Mine call me Mama and they like living here."

Polly gripped the arms of her chair with white knuckles. "Noah and Evie have also adjusted very well to living with me. You can't offer them the love and care I can."

Ecclestone's expression conveyed regret. "I've no doubt you can love them and supply good care. What you don't offer them is a father. Are either of you engaged or do you have prospects of a groom?"

Merry shook her head. "We don't need a husband to be a family. This is a good environment for them. In back is a lovely, large yard for play. They've made friends with other children and have a wonderful time. Our cook prepares nutritious meals for them. They have nice rooms and we've furnished them with clothes, books, and toys. The men living here are good examples. The children lack for nothing."

Blake leaned forward, his hands flat on his desk. "That's true. Living here is like having several grandparents, each of whom is a solid, law abiding, stable, good influence."

Polly added, "Evie is ill and I've consulted a doctor about her care. She has terrible digestive problems you couldn't possibly address at an orphanage. The fact she was so ill when she arrived proves this. And, at the orphanage she was punished for her health problems. Noah is settling in very well, and I believe he'll resume speaking in the near future."

Ecclestone let the papers dangle from his hand. "You don't understand, ladies and Mr. Woolf. I have to follow rules and they clearly state that there must be a married man and woman to take charge of the children who are adopted. You cannot provide that, so I must take the children elsewhere. It's in their best interest."

Merry grabbed the arms of her chair. "How can you say that

when we just told you the excellent care they're receiving here? My sister just told you how much better health her two are in now that they're in her care. Single mothers successfully raise children every day."

Ecclestone shook his head. "I must follow procedure. I assure you the rules were made with the children's welfare in mind. That's why I follow up on each adoption."

Merry leapt to her feet. "You have your nerve, you hypocrite! Where were you when Polly and I were adopted by the meanest couple in Nebraska? No one checked on us. No one! We shared a living hell from the time we were adopted until our so-called parents died almost ten years later. You call that having our welfare in mind?'

Polly shook her finger at Ecclestone. "Having a married couple didn't offer any protection for us. Having a so-called father for the boys adopted at the same time as us didn't keep them from having scars on their backs from the beatings from the man you say is necessary. Merry and I weren't protected when our hands were so raw they bled and we had to huddle together to keep from freezing on winter nights."

Merry leaned over the minister, barely restraining herself from striking the man. "Where were you when we couldn't go to school in bad weather because we didn't have warm enough clothes and no coats? Can you imagine how cold we were doing chores in winter without a coat? You listen to me, you can't take our children, do you hear? *They are our children!*"

Ecclestone, who had leaned as far back in his chair as he could, held up a hand to stay Merry. "Obviously, you were a victim of our system. That was before I was the one verifying parents. I sincerely regret the treatment you received, but you must understand this is why we check each adoptee. I have to check the other children adopted here in Mockingbird Flats. That will take several days. I… I'll give you a week to find a husband before I remove your five children."

She yelled, "A week? One week?"

He waved the same hand. "That's all I can offer. Now, I'd like to go to my room."

Merry jerked open the door. "Don't be late for supper."

She closed the door behind him with a bang and turned toward Blake. "Well, are you able to do anything but referee?"

Polly clasped her hands together. "There must be something you can do to stop him stealing our children."

Blake cleared his throat, his expression pensive. "Since you received the letter, I've thoroughly researched your case. There's simply nothing I can do. Believe me, I'm truly sorry."

Polly pulled her handkerchief from her pocket and dabbed at her weeping eyes. "I must see about Evie." She left the office.

Merry wanted to sink to the floor and curl into a ball. Instead, she clasped her hands, tears stinging the back of her eyelids. "Thank you for letting us meet in your office. I didn't want to chance the children overhearing."

"You're welcome. By the way, that wasn't a volcanic fit. My youngest sister, who you'll soon meet, can shake the walls."

She forced a smile she didn't feel. "Do you know when they're arriving?"

"Tomorrow at three." He gestured to a corner where bedding and a cot waited. "That woman with the unbelievable orange hair brought me supplies."

"Dora Farris is her name and that's her real hair color. She's very nice but she hasn't trusted men since her husband abandoned her ten years ago."

"Nice to know it's not just me she hates. Anyway, you've cleared up another thing. I can't imagine any woman choosing that hair color."

"Thank you again. I've taken enough of your time." She left his office and went to her suite.

She'd almost asked him to marry her. She knew he liked her and had caught him watching her. Why couldn't he propose to her and solve her problems? Good heavens, he lived and worked here anyway so there really wouldn't be much of an adjustment for him.

Chapter Twelve

Merry went to her sister's rooms and caught her weeping. "Polly, I hate seeing you so unhappy."

Polly sniffed and dabbed at her eyes.

"Polly, what are you going to do? Have you thought of someone you can trust as a husband—even temporarily?"

Her sister shook her head. "With that Ecclestone here, I'm sure he'd check to make sure we were sleeping in the same bed. Otherwise, I could ask Gideon or John or Bass."

"Um, Calvin overheard Bass say he's married. Even though his wife left him to live with her parents years ago, they aren't divorced. Still, that leaves Gideon and John."

Polly twisted her handkerchief in her hands. "I have until Friday. I won't lose my children, Merry. I can't. I love them and they love and need me. But, I won't lose our livelihood either by marrying someone I can't trust."

"I know you won't, Polly, and neither will I."

Polly shook her head. "I want to adopt the children officially myself. They're my children." She covered her face with her hands. "I don't know what to do, who to ask." She sobbed until her shoulders shook.

Merry's heart broke seeing her sister so distressed. She pulled her sister's head to her shoulder and held her, patting her back.

Vivid memories of their childhood resurrected. How many times had one or the other or both of them sobbed like this over their situation? She couldn't possibly count the times they'd lost all hope.

The Birds had threatened severe reprisal against those left if one of them ran away. She and Polly lived in constant terror. Bart and Newt only stayed to protect her and Polly, for the boys could have more easily struck out on their own.

Those times were gone and she tried to erase them from her

mind. Events like this brought them back. She'd even dreamed of the bad times after Mr. Ecclestone's letter arrived.

She soothed her sister. "Get it out of your system while the children are outside. You mustn't let them see you cry."

Polly shuddered then pulled away. "I haven't, but it's been difficult. I think I can face them now without tears."

Merry wrung a cloth in water from the pitcher. "Put this on your eyes for a few minutes."

The door opened and Evie and Noah came in.

Evie hurried to Polly. "Is something wrong with you, Mama?"

Polly smiled for the children. "Not now. I had a bit of a headache but your Aunt Merry gave me this cool cloth for my eyes and forehead and it worked like magic."

"We came so I can get my dolly to show Mary Elizabeth."

Noah made motions with his hands.

"He wants me to hurry so we can go play." She carried her doll as she left.

After the children had gone, Merry asked, "She looks stronger today. Is she feeling better?"

"Not really. It seems the more she eats the worse she feels. Mostly she lives on milk and tea. Seems to me she's been able to keep down meat and most vegetables. Any cake or bread comes right back up."

"I'm confident you'll find out what's wrong with her so she can grow healthy and stronger."

"I pray so several times a day. And, that I'll find a good husband who'll marry me and then go away and leave me with the children and the boardinghouse."

"Maybe if you went for a walk or sat on the bench in the back yard you'd get your mind on something more pleasant. Or, you could go see Bea for a visit."

"Perhaps you're right. I'll go visit her at the confectionary shop."

"That will do you good, Polly."

***

Carrying Tammie on her hip an hour later, Merry stared at her

69

sister. "You don't even know this man. Are you positive you want to marry someone you've only briefly met?"

"I explained he needs a wife to inherit his ranch. Really, it's an ideal arrangement. As soon as Mr. Ecclestone witnesses the marriage is valid, Ford will go to his ranch and show the marriage certificate to his grandfather. Then, we'll apply for an annulment."

"How can you be sure this Ford person will actually go away and grant you an annulment?"

"Don't worry, Merry. He doesn't want to get married any more than I do. We're both victims of circumstance. This marriage will allow me to keep the children and allow him to claim his ranch. What could be better?"

"I hope you're right. I'm as desperate as you are. I'm glad one of us has found a solution."

"Do you mind if I leave the children here? I don't want to raise false hopes of a father joining us by having them at the ceremony."

"Under the circumstances, that's probably wise." Merry hugged her sister. "I hope everything works out as you wish."

Polly hurried to meet her groom. Merry hugged her youngest daughter as she watched her sister stride with purpose down the walk. One of them was safe but what was she to do?

She checked on the rest of the children playing in the back yard. Abigail rushed to get Tammie to be the baby in the make believe house she and Mary Elizabeth and Evie had drawn on the ground. Calvin, Noah, and Abraham climbed trees.

How wonderful the five got along so well together now that they were siblings and cousins. The children's laughter strengthened her resolve to find a groom. She had chosen the man, if she had nerve to propose to him.

Chapter Thirteen

Merry was waiting when Polly and Ford Daily returned to the boardinghouse after their wedding. John Allsup was with them.

Polly presented Mr. Ecclestone with her marriage certificate. "Here's the proof you need, Mr. Ecclestone. May I introduce you to my husband, Manford Daily. His friends and family call him Ford."

Mr. Ecclestone peered at the certificate as if he doubted its veracity. "Well, well, this looks to be in order. All right, Mr. and Mrs. Daily, I'll authorize the adoption of Noah Daily and Evelyn Daily. You need to sign here and here."

Looking triumphant, Polly signed then stepped aside for Ford to do so. Afterward, they followed Merry into her suite.

Merry hugged Polly then kissed Ford on the cheek. "Tell me about the wedding. Why was John with you?"

Polly glanced at Ford then at Merry. "You wouldn't believe it, Merry. I'll tell you all about it. First I want to check on the children. Remember, not a word to them about the wedding."

When her sister started toward the back door, Merry called, "Noah and Evie went to their rooms. Evie wanted to rest for a little while."

Ford said, "I'll go up with you, Polly. I'm all packed to leave as soon as I fetch my valise and saddlebags."

Merry hummed as she tidied her rooms. She loved the boardinghouse residents like family, but sometimes she enjoyed being alone in her own private part of the establishment.

Polly rushed in. "They've gone, Merry. Evie and Noah have run away."

Merry shook her head. "But they were just here. How can you be sure?"

"Bass saw them by the Red Dog Saloon not long ago. Ford's gone to saddle our horses. We're going after them. Oh, it's all that horrid Mr. Ecclestone's fault."

"No, Polly. It's ours, mostly mine, for breaking the rules. I don't regret it for a minute. Our children needed us and still do. You find your two."

When Polly and Ford had gone after Noah and Evie, Merry decided the time had come to safeguard hers. Before she lost her nerve, Merry walked to Blake's office. He looked up expectantly as she closed the door behind her.

"Blake Woolf, why don't you and I marry? We could have a paper marriage? After the children are securely mine you could get an annulment."

He stood up and came around his desk then gently grasped her shoulders. "If we marry, it will be permanent and a real marriage. Can you live with that?"

Could she? He appeared to be a nice man. He cared for his mother. His uncle spoke highly of him.

"How could I be sure you wouldn't throw me out of the boardinghouse?"

He shook his head, a perplexed expression on his handsome face. "Surely you know I wouldn't do anything like that. But, I'd live in your suite and work in my office." He tipped her chin up to meet his gaze. "Merry, I'd also share your bed. Can you accept that?"

Merry clutched her throat with one hand. She had to admit being attracted to him. She thought she could trust him. The children liked him. "I… I guess that's only fair. I'll inform Mr. Ecclestone. Shall we marry while your sister and her husband are here?"

"Please. I'd say give my mother a day to recover from her trip then we marry the next day. Do you plan to have the wedding at church or here?"

"Let's have it here so Mrs. Adams and Letitia can easily participate. How about eight o'clock in the evening?"

"Good enough. You arrange it. I'll talk to the preacher."

"I suppose we'll have that awful Mr. Ecclestone attend."

He held her arms. "Merry, I understand your frustration. He's not responsible for what happened to you and Polly. Wrong as he is about you two, he's doing his job the best he can."

She rested her hands on his broad chest. "I know he isn't to blame for the horrid life we had. However, he should be able to make exceptions now. He should realize that single mothers raise independent and well-adjusted children all over the world."

"He's a man who sees the world in black and white and you and Polly are in a gray area."

He brushed a stray lock of hair from her face. "Now, since we're engaged, I want to seal our arrangement with a kiss."

Mesmerized, she watched his mouth as he leaned down to press his lips to hers. Warm tingles shot through her body. Apparently of their own will, her hands clutched at his lapels, pulling him closer.

His legs shifted and he deepened the kiss. He molded his body to hers, caressing her back. When he ended the kiss, he kept her close and tucked her head beneath his chin.

His heart pounded wildly beneath her ear. "That was some kiss, Miss Bird."

She hung on to him, her heart racing fast as his while she nestled her head against his strong chest. "I don't have a comparison, but I must agree, Mr. Woolf."

Now that her knees weren't threatening to give way, she took a step from him. "I-I'll go tell the children."

He grinned, his eyes shining with mischief. "Whew, I'll try to recover from that kiss. Then, I'll go talk to the preacher. Perhaps we can announce our engagement at supper."

Safe. Her children were safe. Relief carried her to her suite.

***

Blake sat at his desk for half an hour to recover his composure and consider the commitment he'd just made. Had he lost his mind? Only lately had he escaped family responsibilities. Now he was back in the fray.

Mulling over his predicament, he vowed he'd done the right thing. He should have proposed to Merry when she received the letter from the Children's Aid Society. At the same time, he couldn't believe he was soon to be married with three children.

Rising and clamping his hat on his head, he strode out the office's front door toward the parsonage. He rapped on the preacher's door.

Sara Jones answered, one hand patting her brown hair in place. "Why, come in, Mr. Woolf. How nice to see you. I'll let my husband know you're here. He's just returned from visiting an ailing member of the congregation."

She gestured to a chair. "Please have a seat."

By now, Blake would have exploded if he'd sat still to await Reverend Jones. The small parlor hardly allowed room for pacing, but Blake managed.

The preacher came in with his hand extended and wearing his usual broad smile. "Nice of you to call. What can I do for you?"

Blake shook hands then shifted from one foot to the other. "Miss Merry Bird and I would like you to perform our marriage ceremony." There, he'd said it. Too late to back out now.

The other man clapped him on the back. "Wonderful. Having recently performed the ceremony for Miss Polly and her groom, I hoped you were here for this reason. I can't tell you how much you've relieved my mind."

The preacher sat in one of the armchairs. "Yesterday I had a note from Mr. Ecclestone and it upset me so much I hardly slept a wink last night. I know how much the Bird sisters love those children and how happy the children are now."

Blake sat in the other armchair. "They've settled in and appear happy. I'd hate like he…heck to have them uprooted."

"I sense urgency. When is this wedding to take place?"

"As it happens, my mother and sister are arriving tomorrow and mother will be living at the boardinghouse." Blake told him the arrangements.

The minister nodded his agreement to the plans. "Sounds as if you've thought of everything."

Reverend Jones leaned forward, concern etched on his face. "Please don't misunderstand me when I spoke of Grover Ecclestone's note upsetting me. He's a fine man with high principles who does a lot of good. Has he arrived yet?"

Blake raised his eyebrows. "Oh, yes, he's made himself known. He's staying at the boardinghouse."

He couldn't keep a wry smile from his face. "You should have seen Merry confront him about the horrid way she and her sister were treated by the couple who adopted them. I believe that's why he decided to give them a week to marry before he told the children they have to return to the orphanage."

The minister steepled his fingers on his abdomen. "I had no idea they'd had a difficult life. Miss Merry is always so cheerful and positive. One would think she'd never had anything unpleasant happen or had a bad thought."

Blake all but snorted. "Hard to believe anyone would treat a child the way she and Polly and the two boys adopted with them were treated. The girls were only eight when they went to live with that Bird couple in Nebraska. They worked like slaves and didn't even have coats to wear in winter. Worked until their hands were raw and bleeding."

Reverend Jones frowned and shook his head slowly. "Sad as that sounds, I've heard similar stories. Most adoptees at least get good food and care. However, if you compare even minimal nurturing to the dangers of living on the streets of New York, then they're better off."

Blake supposed so but no better than in an orphanage. "Children need to feel wanted and protected. Merry and Polly have given their five love and security."

Blake stood. "I didn't mean to go on and on. I'll see you at the wedding. I hope Mrs. Jones will be able to attend as well."

The minister walked him the short distance to the door. "We'll be there. How fortunate that your mother and sister will be able to see you wed. I'll look forward to meeting your family."

Blake strolled the few blocks toward the boardinghouse. The engine's whistle sounded as another train rolled into town. Tomorrow, part of his family would arrive and in three days, he'd be a married man.

Before he announced his engagement to Merry, he wanted to talk to the children—especially Calvin and Abigail.

Back at the boardinghouse, he detoured to the back. Sure enough, the two older children were playing with friends.

When Abigail spotted him, she ran over and took his hand.

"Did you come to take us for more of that sar'prilla?"

"Not today, but sometime soon we'll get some." He motioned to Calvin as he guided Abigail toward a bench in the shade of a tall cottonwood tree. A breeze rustled the leaves and a blue jay called, the combination creating nature's music.

Calvin had lost only a little of his defensive attitude. He stood in front of Blake and crossed his arms. "Mama said you're gonna marry her. I didn't tell her I asked you to, did you?"

"No, that was between us. I came to see how you two feel about me marrying your Mama."

Calvin's solemn expression still resembled that of a much older person. "It's a good plan. I was afraid we were gonna be taken away from Mama by that Mr. Ecclestone. Mama doesn't know I read that man's letter."

Blake sensed a frown form on his forehead. "You know reading someone else's private correspondence is not proper, Calvin. She'd be disappointed if she knew."

The boy bowed his head until his chin almost touched his chest. "Like I told you, I only did it because I heard her crying. She's a real good person and she oughtn't to have anything bad happen to her."

Calvin raised his chin. "She was sitting on the couch in our part of the house and she had a piece of paper in her hand. I can be real quiet, see, so she didn't know I was peeking out of my room. When she went to her bedroom, she was still crying. I slipped out to see what was so bad."

Blake nodded. "I can understand your urge to spy. I saw the letter, too. Your mama and Miss Polly were very upset."

"Then you know that man from the Children's Aid Society was gonna take us back to the orphanage." Calvin crossed his arms. "I ain't going back."

"I don't blame you. Now that your mama and I will be married, you're safe from the orphanage. Once she and I are wed, no one can take you from us. Still, I wanted to be sure her marrying me would be all right with you."

"I'm glad you're gettin' hitched. Mama needs a husband.

76

Abigail and Tammie need a pa."

Abigail leaned against his shoulder. "You'll be our Papa, won't you? I don't know if I had a Papa before."

Blake smiled at the little girl who would soon be his daughter. "You'll also have a Grandma because my mother is coming here to live. She'll be happy to have you two and Tammie as her grandchildren."

Abigail's eyes widened. "She will?"

Calvin sat beside him. "I kinda remember having a Ma and I told you I had a Pa 'til I was eight, but I never had a grandma or grandpa."

"You'll have a grandmother now. She'll arrive tomorrow. My father passed away years ago, so I can't supply a grandfather."

Abigail cried, "Tammie." She sprang up and ran to where Merry approached carrying Tammie.

Merry sat beside him and set Tammie down to play.

Abigail held the toddler's shoulders. "Tammie, did you know he's going to be our new Papa."

Tammie climbed up into his lap and patted his face. "Papa. My papa."

He was amazed at Tammie's reaction. "That's right, sunshine. I'll be your papa and you and Abigail will be my little girls and Calvin will be my son."

Merry was silent.

He reached for her hand and laced their fingers. "Preacher is arranged. Anything else I'm supposed to take care of before the ceremony?" Dadgum, he had to get her a ring.

"I think we're all set. Elvira plans to bake a wedding cake. W-We can announce our plans at supper this evening."

Chapter Fourteen

Blake had his own plans for supper. Mr. Ecclestone was seated in Bass' chair. When everyone else was gathered and Merry was in the dining room, Blake walked over to her.

He took hold of Merry's hand and dropped to one knee. "Merry Bird, will you do me the honor of becoming my wife?"

She gasped, her beautiful blue eyes wide, and stammered, "I... I... Yes, Blake, I'll be honored."

He stood and kissed her cheek while everyone in the dining room clapped. He escorted her to the table where the children waited. She'd acquired a high chair for Tammie, so the fourth seat was available.

He held Merry's chair. "I suppose we'll have to change arrangements so we dine together."

She smiled at him but he saw moisture gathered in her eyes. "That was nice of you, Blake. Thank you."

Dora set a plate of food in front of Blake. "You're our hero, and I'll make sure you get the biggest dessert every meal from here on in."

She also set a plate in front of Merry and Calvin. Blake didn't know how she could carry plates lined up on her arm without dropping them.

Calvin offered the widest grin Blake had seen on the boy's face. "Now we'll be a real family."

Merry patted her son's arm. "Everything will work out now. I feel years younger than I did this morning."

Blake wasn't sure he did. He was relieved the drama with Merry and her three was taken care of. At the same time, he'd made a lifetime commitment at a period in his life when he needed to be unhampered by a family.

Add that to the fact his mother was moving here and he figured he was touched in the head. Observing the happiness on Merry's face and that of Calvin and Abigail, he reckoned he could live with his decision. When his mind strayed to nights with the beautiful Merry, he wasn't even tempted to go back on his word.

***

The following afternoon Blake hurried to the train station. He'd arranged with Yancey Cameron to show up for his mother's trunk. He saw Yancey's wagon parked as near the platform as he could get the horses and vehicle.

Blake shifted from one foot to the other as the train pulled up to the depot. He saw his flighty little sister step down from the train instead of helping their mother. He rushed forward as his mother appeared. At least Hector held her arm.

Leaning down, he kissed her cheek. "Ma, I'm so glad you're here. How was your trip?"

"Lovely and very exciting. I'd never ridden the train, you know."

He shook hands with his new relative. "Congratulation, Hector, and welcome to the family."

Jessie put her hands on her hips. "I suppose you're so mad at me you aren't going to wish me well?"

"I'm plenty angry with you but I do wish you well." In spite of his irritation, he kissed his sister's cheek. "Ma will be better off here than in Jefferson."

He signaled to Yancey. "Ma, this is Yancey Cameron and he'll get your trunk if you give him your receipt."

Yancey took charge of the claim ticket and the suitcases before he went for the trunk.

When Yancey had gone on his way, Blake offered his arm to his mother. "The boardinghouse is only a short ways. Do you feel well enough to walk?"

"I'm not an invalid, son. After sitting all this time, a short walk will be welcome."

He strolled slowly and let his mother set the pace. "I have big news to tell you, Ma. Yesterday, I became engaged to Merry Bird, one of the owners of the boardinghouse. She has three children she adopted from the orphan train last month."

His mother beamed at him. "I'm so happy for you. I can hardly wait to meet her and the children. How old are they?"

"No one knows for sure but as near as they can guess, Calvin is nine, Abigail is six, and Tammie is almost two. They're looking forward to having a grandmother."

Jessie swished ahead. "I guess that leaves you sitting pretty, doesn't it? Now you own Uncle George's law practice, all the money he left, and a boardinghouse."

His mother said, "Jessie, there is no call to be spiteful, especially after Blake paid your and Hector's way here."

She huffed, "I just think Uncle George could have split his money among all of us instead of it all going to Blake."

Hector tried put his arm around her waist but she stomped ahead. He turned back. "Sorry, Blake, Jessie don't much like living with my parents. Mama insists she help with the housework and Jessie thought she'd be treated like a guest."

Blake grimaced. "Frankly, Hector, there wasn't much money left and I've reserved it for Ma's care. Afraid you and your folks have a tough time cut out for you for the next few months. Reckon Jessie will grow up and settle down eventually."

Hector stuffed his hands in his pockets. "I sure hope so. I love her and I figure she loves me but she sure is pig-headed."

His mother said, "She's spoiled rotten is the problem. You and I are partly to blame, son. Added to that is she got your father's stubbornness."

He gestured ahead. "There it is, Ma. The big yellow building up ahead is the boardinghouse. My office is at the front on the east end."

"My, that is a lovely building and so large. How many people live there?"

He'd meant to ask but kept forgetting. "You know, I'm not sure. A couple of the men are traveling salesmen only there part of the time. I hope you like living there as much as I do."

His sister stood at the entrance to the boardinghouse, arms crossed and tapping her foot.

80

Blake guided his mother up the walk. She stopped to look at the sign that said *Davis Law Office*. "Oh, there's where George had his office and now it's yours. Poor brother should have lived for years longer."

"I'll probably change the name someday. A Mr. Nevins is coming early next week to add my name below that wording."

"Oh, yes, your name should be there."

Merry opened the front door as they came up the steps. "Welcome to Mockingbird Flats Boardinghouse. I'm Merry Bird."

His mother hugged her. "I'm so happy to hear the news of your engagement to my son."

Blake introduced his sister and her husband.

Yancey came down the stairs. "All tucked in place, Mr. Woolf."

Blake passed him his fee plus a bit extra. "Thank you."

"Thank you." Yancey shot out the door.

Merry took his mother's arm. "Perhaps you'd like to refresh yourself in my room and wait until after supper to climb the stairs and see where you'll live."

"If you don't mind, I'll do that. Maybe having stairs to climb will strengthen my legs in the coming months."

Blake doubted that. "Since Merry is taking care of you, Ma, I'll show Jessie and Hector where they'll be staying." He headed for the stairs.

Jessie and Hector's voices carried to him, her complaining and him placating her.

At the top of the stairs, Blake turned right and opened his door. "Here you are. This is my room and I'd appreciate it if you don't mess about with my stuff."

Hector eyed the bed and then Jessie longingly. "Where will you sleep?"

Blake fought to keep from rolling his eyes. Poor Hector couldn't get Jessie alone in his room soon enough.

"On a cot in my office until after the wedding in two days. Thought we'd have the wedding while you two are here."

His sister appeared mollified by the news. "That's nice of you.

81

I'm glad we'll be able to attend. I hope what I brought to wear will be presentable enough."

"I'm sure it will. You always look nice. Now, if you'll excuse me, I'll go see about Ma and make sure she doesn't need anything from her room."

Blake was happy to escape his petulant sister and her lustful husband. Poor Hector had no idea he would have to be tougher or be henpecked for the rest of his life. Downstairs, Blake knocked on the door of Merry's suite.

She answered. "Come in. Your mother is having a cup of tea."

He followed her while scanning his surroundings. This is where he'd be living in the future. He was met with soothing colors and comfortable appearing furnishings he could enjoy.

His mother sat in an upholstered chair with her feet on a hassock. She held a cup of tea with the saucer on the side table. Abigail leaned on the chair's arm and Tammie sat on the floor.

Calvin actually smiled. "Your mother said we can call her Grandma."

Ma said, "And what else would you call me, dear, when that's what I'll be? I'm pleased to have three lovely grandchildren right here where I can see you each day."

Calvin stood in front of Blake. "Wanna see my room? It's just mine and nobody else sleeps there."

"Certainly." Blake followed the boy who was soon to be his son.

Calvin opened the door and stood back. "See, I have my own toys. Clothes, too, but I put them away. Mama said 'fore long I can choose the colors for a new bed quilt and paper on the walls."

Blake was impressed. "You keep it neat, that's good."

Abigail tugged on his hand. "Come see my room and Tammie's."

Blake let her lead him next door. He whispered, "I see your doll and the bear are asleep."

She giggled. He picked her up and carried her back where his mother sat. He joined Merry on the couch with Abigail on his lap. Looking happier than he'd ever seen the boy, Calvin plopped on the floor and crossed his legs. Tammie climbed on Merry's lap.

Ma's eyes sparkled and she beamed at him. "I'm so happy to see you settled. Thank you for waiting until I could attend the ceremony. Seeing you wed means a lot to me."

Merry glanced at him. "We're glad you'll be living here, too. We function like an extended family. Don't let Mrs. Adams or Miss Cross intimidate you. They're really good-hearted but they take getting used to."

Ma chuckled. "That does sound like a family. One or two always need a little more attention."

He nodded. "How many people actually live here, Merry? I've never counted."

She smiled and gestured at Ma. "Including your mother, the staff, children, residents, and those who are only here part of the time, there are twenty-seven of us. We often have to turn away people who want to live here but I'm not sure we could manage many more even if we had more rooms."

He laid his arm on the couch behind Merry's shoulders. "Appears to work well. I've heard no complaints. The men I've been eating with tell me you've improved their lives since you and Polly came."

"How nice to hear they said so. True we've made improvements as we're able. We're cautious in case something changes."

The gong's loud clang reverberated through the air.

His mother almost dropped her cup. "What was that?" Fortunately she'd finished her tea so nothing spilled.

Merry rose and took the china from his mother. "I should have warned you. Elvira Koch, our cook, rings the gong to call us to supper. It's just outside this room so it's loud. Has to be for those on the third floor to hear."

His mother got to her feet and brushed at her skirts. "Startled me is all because I wasn't expecting it. I'm sure I'll get used to it."

Calvin stepped forward. "Grandma, I can show you where we sit."

Merry glanced at Blake. "We can scoot two tables together so there's room for everyone in the family."

They filed into the dining room. At least Jessie had lost her petulant expression. Blake remembered her as a sweet child. Had she always been so selfish and he only noticed since he'd been away from her for a few weeks?

A FAMILY FOR MERRY

Chapter Fifteen

When his mother was ready to retire, Blake escorted her to her room with Merry leading the way. Jessie followed him but Hector turned off and went to his room. Blake had to admit he was curious about where Ma would be living.

By the time they reached the top of the two sets of stairs, his mother had slowed considerably and pressed a hand on her lower abdomen.

"You all right, Ma?"

"Fine, son." But she wasn't convincing.

How would she be able to do this several times every day? He would like to believe her legs would strengthen but he couldn't. Someone would have to escort her and even then, as now, she'd have difficulty.

When they reached the third floor hallway, his mother heaved a sigh. Merry opened the door to a room and stood back for them to enter.

Ma stopped in the doorway. "Oh, how lovely and what a nice large size." She sank onto the armchair by the window and peered at her surroundings.

The walls had cabbage roses in various shades on a blue background. The rug went to within a foot or so of the walls. A blue quilt covered the bed. The furniture was golden oak and included a four poster bed, washstand, armoire, night table, and chest as well as the chair and lamp table.

Merry poured Ma a glass of water from the pitcher. "When one of the suites becomes available, you can move into that. The Randalls are saving to buy a home so their stay here is temporary."

"This is lovely, Merry. I couldn't ask for a nicer room."

Merry appeared worried. "Your windows overlook the back yard. I do hope the sound of the children playing won't disturb you."

85

Ma laughed. "The sound of children having fun has always been music to my ears."

Jessie looked around. "I wish we had a room this nice at Hector's. Ours is tiny compared to this."

Ma shook her finger at Jessie. "Jessie Evans, don't you go looking down your nose at what your husband provides for you. You chose him and his parents' home. They could have refused to let you live with them and then you and Hector would be in trouble. Be grateful Mr. and Mrs. Evans have accepted you into their family."

Jessie gaped at her. "Ma?"

"You heard me. Now you go on to Hector and quit complaining."

His sister looked as if their mother had slapped her. She puckered up to cry but he guided her out the door.

"Enjoy your trip while you can, Jessie. Tomorrow you can look around town. The wedding is day after that and then the next day you'll head home."

She sent him a sly glance. "Maybe Hector and I could live here instead of on the farm."

He shook his head. "Don't think you can mooch off Ma or me. You've made your choice, now live with the result. Hector deserves your loyalty and support. He also deserves more respect from you and less complaining." He swatted her rear and aimed her at the stairs.

She had tears in her eyes when she glanced back at him but she was silent. His sister letting someone else have the last word was new.

Back in his mother's room, he leaned over and kissed her cheek. "Ma, I'll let you get settled and see you in the morning. You rest easy."

Ma smiled but he could tell she was overly tired. "Goodnight, son. Goodnight, Merry."

When they reached the parlor, Mr. Ecclestone was coming in the front door with his briefcase in his hand.

"I've had a busy but satisfying day. I met with the Bushnells, the Canups, and the Zimmermans about the children they're adopting. All nice families and the children have settled in and appear happy and well treated."

Merry straightened her spine. "Reverend Jones guarded the front door of the church while the children were being selected. He wouldn't have let an unsatisfactory couple take children."

Mr. Ecclestone peered at her over his spectacles. "I see. Well, tomorrow I'll check some rural families. Goodnight."

After the man had gone upstairs, Merry laid a hand on Blake's arm. "I think we should pool our funds and build on to this suite for your mother. Those stairs were difficult for her and will only become more so over the years."

"An excellent idea. Are you certain you wouldn't mind?"

"I've sketched it out in my mind, a large room with a sitting area. We can talk about the details later."

"Thank you, Merry, for being so considerate. I don't want you to think I'm a mama's boy who'll pander to her and neglect you. Far from it, but I'm the eldest and feel responsible for her welfare."

"That's to your credit. She appears to be a delightful person. I'm looking forward to finally having a real mother."

"That's a kind thing to say." Blake kissed Merry goodnight.

Having her in his arms ignited base urges he'd thought he could control. He was no better than Hector for he longed to take Merry to bed this minute.

He had intended the kiss to be a gentle goodnight. When his mouth covered hers, blood pounded and his body came alive. Any doubts he'd had about this union fled in the knowledge that this beautiful, intelligent woman would soon be his wife. His to hold and caress to their hearts' content.

***

The next morning Merry was busy in preparation for the wedding that would happen the following day. She cleared out half of the storage in her room to allow for Blake's things. The thought of sharing a bed with him sent mixed ripples through her body.

Warm tingles reminded her of the astonishing goodnight kiss they'd shared. She'd wanted the kiss to go on and on forever. Knowing he'd be sharing her body created heat that pooled in her lower abdomen yet also generated wariness.

Yesterday when they were on the couch in her suite—soon to

be *their* suite of rooms—Blake's arm along her shoulders had been reassuring, supportive. She thought again of his kiss and her fingers went to her lips.

Of course she knew the basic facts of coupling. After all, she'd grown up on a farm where animals were occasionally bred. Cattle mating had appeared painful and brutal for the cow. Was that how it was with people?

Who could she ask? Bea Quentin had married Steve Upton only last week but she'd never get a chance to talk to her alone at the confectionary shop. Sue Travis or Eunice Randall might talk to her about coming together with a man.

In the meantime, she had to get her dress chosen and pressed as well as clothes ready for her children. Suddenly, she thought she'd swoon. She trusted Blake but the thought of placing her life in his control set her heart racing and her head spinning. She dropped onto a chair before she could fall.

Abigail ran to her. "What's wrong, Mama? Are you sick like Evie gets?"

With cheer she didn't feel, she smiled at her daughter. "I'm fine, dear. I was making a list in my head of all we have to do today and tomorrow to get ready for us marrying your new Papa."

"Are there lots of things?"

"Not too many to finish in time. Nothing you have to do except tell me which dress you want to wear for the wedding."

Abigail clapped her hands. "The blue one is my favorite. Tammie has a blue one too. We can be twins."

She touched the tip of her sweet daughter's nose with a fingertip. "I'm going to wear a blue dress, so we'll be triplets."

Abigail ran to Calvin's room. "What are you going to wear to Mama's wedding?"

Calvin shrugged. "Whatever Mama tells me to wear. Us men don't care that much about clothes."

Merry suppressed a laugh. Her son identified with Blake as if they were the same age. She was glad Calvin admired his soon-to-be father and had chosen him as a role model.

She wrote her list and would cross things off as she

88

accomplished them. Doing so gave her a sense of completion—when everything on the list was crossed out, she'd have achieved her daily goal. In addition, she'd be as prepared as she could for her wedding. At least physically, but how was she to prepare her mind and heart?

The answer was, she couldn't. Simply put, there was no way she could get ready for an experience as foreign to her as riding a shooting star.

Abigail tugged at her sleeve. "Mama, you still look sad."

She pulled her daughter onto her lap. "Oh, no, sweetheart. So much is happening my mind can't take it all in."

Abigail pondered. "I don't know anything about getting married. You should ask Grandma to help. I'll bet she can tell you."

"Of course, that's a wonderful idea." She set Abigail on her feet and then stood. "Would you like to go play or come to the parlor with me?"

"I'm going to play house with Mary Elizabeth but I needed my dolly."

"Have fun with your friends."

When Abigail had gone outside, Merry pocketed her list, picked up Tammie, and went to the parlor. Blake's mother, who had insisted she call her Ma, sat with Mrs. Adams, Letitia, and Eunice. They were engrossed in what appeared to be companionable conversation.

"Ladies, I'm going to the emporium for a few things for the reception. Do either of you need anything?"

She received a no from each woman.

"Ma, would you like to come along?"

Ma smiled at the ladies near her then looked at Merry. "I'm enjoying visiting with these ladies and resting up from my trip. I hope you won't mind if I wait and go with you another time. Perhaps you'd like to leave Tammie with me." She held out her arms and Tammie reached for her.

"That's a good girl, come to Grandma." Ma cradled Tammie in her lap.

"Thank you, Ma. This will make my trip easier and faster."

Merry was actually glad she could go on this errand alone.

When she'd reviewed her nightwear, she realized she had nothing suitable for a wedding night. She hoped no one would see her choose what she wanted.

Even though this was not a typical marriage, Blake had insisted he wanted a real marriage in every way. That meant he would see her tonight and the nights to come as she came to bed.

At the emporium, she thought she could swoop in, pick out a pretty nightgown, and go home. No sooner was she inside than Jane Dorchester, one of the owners, came over. At least it wasn't Sam Randall from the boardinghouse. She waved at him then looked away so he wouldn't come to help her.

Jane said, "I understand you're engaged. Roy and I are happy for you. What can I help you with today?"

As quietly as she could, Merry said, "A nightgown."

Jane gestured to the right and spoke as if announcing to the entire town. "Nightgowns are right over here. I'll bet you want something special for your wedding night and honeymoon."

She turned her back to the two men who worked there. "We're not going on a honeymoon. I just need something new to wear at night. Those I have are worn and no longer pretty."

"How about this one to tempt your groom?" Jane held up a daring gown that was all but transparent and dipped very low in front and back.

Merry's face heated in a blush. "No, um, don't you have something more, um, modest?"

Jane's eyes sparkled. "No need to be embarrassed, dear. After all, you want to appeal to your husband. Well, look at this one of lawn."

Merry held this offering. "The lace would be scratchy for sleeping." She handed it back to Jane. "I had in mind something with ribbon trim and maybe a ruffle on the bottom."

The store owner sighed, as if she thought Merry was hard to please. "This cambric gown is lovely. No ruffle but the tucks at the top should be flattering. Blue ribbon bows add a nice touch."

"That's what I want. Do you have another like it or similar?"

Jane pulled another garment from the stack in the cupboard.

90

This gown resembled the one Merry had chosen.

Jane asked, "How do you like this one?"

"Perfect. I'll take both of them."

Merry wished Sam Randall weren't listening to this conversation. Not that he was eavesdropping, but he was working so close that he couldn't help hearing Jane's loud voice. His living at the boardinghouse caused Merry to feel differently than she did about Roy Dorchester.

She paid for her purchase and left.

When she'd returned from the emporium and checked on the children, she pressed her dress. After growing up wearing rags cut down from Ruby Bird's cast offs, she enjoyed pretty clothes. Although she hadn't a large selection of garments, those she had were flattering to her and of good quality.

The dress she'd chosen for her wedding had a deep blue faille skirt. The top's long basque apron had satin pleats underneath and was several shades lighter than the skirt. White duchesse lace edged the square neck and the three-quarter sleeves.

Blake has seen he wear it once to church. He'd complimented her then. Having something to wear that she knew appealed to him created a pleasant sensation.

Oh, bother, she was already trying to please her husband and they weren't married yet.

Chapter Sixteen

All day Thursday, Merry had been on edge. The other residents were as excited as if she were really their kin.

Abigail was flower girl and Calvin was giving her away. In Polly's absence, Jessie was matron of honor. Hector served as best man. Merry and Ma had talked and decided Tammie was too young to be a flower girl with Abigail.

Jessie clutched a small bouquet. "Blake and Hector organized the parlor into rows of seating with an open center aisle. The preacher and his wife are here and ready to start the ceremony. That other man, Mr. Ecclestone, is in the parlor, too."

Merry didn't want Mr. Ecclestone at her wedding. Just the same, he was here. He'd know they were really married, wouldn't he?

Tammie was usually such a pleasant child. When she saw that Abigail had a basket of flowers, she started crying.

"Want flowers," she wailed.

Ma said, "Come sit with me, Tammie."

Instead, Tammie sat on the floor, sobbing.

Abigail begged, "Please, Mama, let Tammie walk with me."

"If we can find something suitable for her to carry." She bent down. "Tammie, do you remember when we practiced and Abigail tossed flower petals on the floor?"

Tammie nodded but Merry was not reassured.

"Will you do just like Abigail does with her rose petals?"

The little girl looked at her sister. "Yeth."

Merry had misgivings but wanted all three children to participate in the wedding. She took out her handkerchief and dried her youngest child's face. Usually Tammie was a good child but she had her own way of doing things.

Elvira rooted around the storeroom and found a small basket Tammie could use. Abigail gave her younger sister half her rose petals. Appeased, Tammie smiled.

Elvira said, "You'd better get on the way before that man changes his mind."

"You're right. Is everyone ready now? Ma, we'll wait until you're seated at the front."

When Ma and Elvira had found seats, Mrs. Jones played Mendelssohn on the piano.

Jessie stood in front of Merry. "Go on girls. Walk slowly and toss your petals on the floor in front of where you're walking."

Their floral scent drifted back to Merry and blended with the fragrance of the bouquet of roses and daisies she carried.

Abigail glided just as they'd practiced and dropped rose petals as she proceeded down the aisle.

Tammie, on the other hand, chose to throw the flowers on those attending. She did so by the handful and added, "Whee." Then she stopped to sort through the basket as if looking for something.

Blake's face contorted with barely suppressed laughter and chuckles filled the room.

Jessie tried to urge Tammie and Abigail forward by putting a hand on Abigail's shoulder.

Abigail turned around and said, "Mama, Aunt Jessie pushed me."

Jessie gave Merry a horrified glance then shrugged.

Calvin looked up at Merry and shook his head.

Merry motioned the girls to move. Eventually, she surrendered and said, "Tammie, Abigail, keep walking to where Papa is standing. Remember what we practiced."

Abigail said, "Come on, Tammie."

Both girls resumed tossing the rose petals. Jessie followed them and then Merry and Calvin walked toward the small lectern set in the doorway of Blake's office. Reverend Jones stood behind the portable lectern and Blake and Hector stood near.

When Blake made eye contact, she realized his eyes held more than humor. He gazed at her as if she were a precious gift. Her legs

93

dissolved and she had to rely on Calvin to keep from falling.

Jessie guided Abigail and Tammie to one side. Calvin and she stopped beside Blake.

Tammie twirled around and then plopped on the floor as if dizzy. Abigail set down her basket and helped Tammie stand up. "We're s'posed to stand here by Aunt Jessie 'til this is over. 'Member how you saw us practice?"

Tammie toyed with her hair bow until it was lopsided and dangling. "Yeth, I 'member now."

Reverend Jones asked, "Who gives this woman in marriage?"

Looking as if he would burst with pride, Calvin announced in a firm, clear voice, "My sisters and I do." Then he gave her hand to Blake before he sat beside his new grandma.

The preacher smiled at Merry, his eyes twinkling as he went through the wedding vows.

When it came her time, he asked, "Do you, Mercedes Murphy Bird, take this man to be your lawfully wedded husband, forsaking all others and cleaving only unto him, to have and to hold from this day forward, for better or worse, for richer or poorer, in sickness and in health, to love, honor, and obey until death do us part."

Her voice quavered as shaky as she was when she answered, "I do."

She'd just promised to obey him when she had no intention of obeying any man as if she were a child unable to think for herself. This wasn't what she'd intended, but hope for the future blossomed in her heart. Perhaps someday Blake would come to care for her. In the meantime, she trusted him to keep his word.

Reverend Jones turned toward Blake. "Do you, Blake George Woolf, take this woman to be your lawfully wedded wife, forsaking all others and cleaving only unto her, to have and to hold from this day forward, for better or for worse, for richer or for poorer, in sickness and in health, to love and to cherish, until death do us part."

Blake's strong baritone reassured her. "I do."

The preacher asked, "Do you have the ring?"

Hector handed Blake a ring then Blake took Merry's hand. "With this ring, I thee wed."

94

Merry gazed down at the gold band on the third finger of her left hand. She was married to this handsome man her children already adored. If she were honest, she shared their opinion.

Reverend Jones smiled at Blake. "You may kiss the bride."

He turned toward her. She sensed this ceremony had deeply affected him as it had her. Yet, when he kissed her, his lips barely brushed hers.

When they touched, a tingle flowed through her body. She couldn't keep her mind from the coming night.

The preacher said, "Please face the guests." When they'd turned, he announced, "I present Mr. and Mrs. Blake Woolf."

He held up his hands for attention. "I've been asked to tell you that there is a reception in the dining room."

She and Blake hurried down the aisle and led the way to the dining room.

Elvira and her helper, Delbert Loving, had slipped out of the ceremony early and were ready to help guests with cake and punch.

During the reception, Mr. Ecclestone cornered Merry and Blake. "I see that you've fulfilled the requirements for keeping the three children you accepted from the orphan train. Odd, I don't see your sister and her groom and family."

Merry tried not to snarl. "My sister, her husband, and the children are on a trip."

He rubbed his hands together. "Of course, a honeymoon. I should have thought of that. I'm surprised the children accompanied them."

Merry neither confirmed nor denied his assumption. "Would you care for more cake, Mr. Ecclestone?"

Merry turned to her husband. "I should toss my bouquet."

Blake tapped a spoon against a glass. "Get ready to catch the bride's bouquet."

Merry grinned and tossed.

Miss Cross caught the flowers. "Oh, my goodness."

Blake chuckled in Merry's ear. "Well aimed, my dear wife."

"Now I need to get the children to bed."

"I'll help. Shall we start with Tammie?" He scooped up the

child and tickled her tummy.

When she stopped laughing, she patted his face. "My papa."

"That's right, Tammie. Now I'm your papa and Abigail's and Calvin's." He carried her to the owner's suite.

Merry followed with Calvin and Abigail. "That went well, don't you think? You did a wonderful job of escorting me, Calvin."

Abigail pulled at Merry's skirt. "What about me, Mama?"

Merry met Blake's gaze. "You were the best flower girl I've ever had. Children, it's past your bedtime. We've had a busy day, so I know you're tired."

Blake passed Tammie to Merry. "All right if I tuck in Calvin and you take the girls?"

Calvin said, "Aw, no one has to put me to bed. I can do it myself."

Merry smiled at her son. "Of course you can, but parents enjoy saying a special goodnight to their children."

Calvin's face registered surprise. "You do?"

Blake loosened his tie as he led the way to Calvin's room. "You don't want me to miss my first opportunity to be your papa, do you?"

With a genuine smile on his face, Calvin hurried toward his room. "No, 'course not."

Merry got the girls into their nightgowns and tucked them into bed. She'd yet to get a small bed for Tammie but vowed to do so this coming week. Surely there would be fewer distractions after tonight.

She thought of one distraction she didn't mind—her handsome husband. How fortunate she was to have Blake and her three children. They were a family, perfect if only Blake cared for her as much as she'd come to care for him.

Why not admit it? She'd fallen in love with the man who was now her husband. Surely there was nothing wrong with that.

When the children were tucked in and asleep, she joined Blake on the couch of the suite's sitting room.

He tilted his head toward the main part of the hotel. "Sounds as if the reception is still in progress. I'm sorry Polly wasn't back in time to take part in the ceremony."

"Thank goodness we had a telegram from them and they're all right. You know, it occurred to me John knows the secrets of everyone in town, yet he never gossips."

"That's a good thing. You sure you're content to miss the rest of the reception?"

"I'm glad we're in here. The evening was lovely, even with Tammie's spontaneous variations to the way we rehearsed. Thank you, Blake, for insuring the children remained here."

"Thank you for allowing me to be a part of your life. You know I didn't want to commit right now but this seems right. In fact, let me show you the surprise I arranged for you."

He scooped her into his arms and carried her to their bedroom. "Not exactly over the threshold but serves the purpose here."

Merry stared around her and inhaled the heavenly fragrance. "This is like being in a garden."

Garlands of flowers were strung from bedpost to bedpost, from the furniture, and the curtain rods. Vases of flowers were on every surface. Rose petals were scattered from the doorway to the bed and across the pillows and the turned back sheets.

He bowed. "Our own leafy bower, created just for you. Not that I did the work, you must know, but Myrtle Smith from the florist shop and Bea Upton commandeered the Bushnell women and sneaked in during the reception."

"That you arranged this for me means so much. I was afraid you had regrets."

He caressed her cheek. "Marrying you is the best thing that's ever happened to me."

She searched his face with her gaze. "Can you mean that? I've worried so that you were feeling trapped for doing your good deed."

He chuckled and pulled her close. "You think I married you to do a good deed? Have you forgotten I couldn't stop watching you whenever we were in the same room? I couldn't stop thinking about you no matter where we were."

Could she have heard him correctly? "Blake, I admit I'm as enamored of you as the children are."

He leaned back and raised his eyebrows. "But not in the same

97

CAROLINE CLEMMONS

way, I hope?"

She smiled and traced a finger across his mouth. "No, not in the least the same way. My feelings are of a far different nature."

He kissed her temple then looked into her eyes. "Tell me how."

"When you're near like this, my brain disconnects and my limbs turn wobbly. I can't help needing your arms around me."

"That's good to hear because I definitely want you near me for the rest of our lives. I've fallen in love with you, Merry Woolf. I hope someday you can learn to feel the same way about me."

"I don't need to learn something I already know. I've fallen in love with you. I suppose I fell for you that day you were so patient with Calvin when he hired you to defend him against the man who killed his father."

"Ah, I thought I saw the shadow of an eavesdropper that day."

He pressed his lips to hers and heat sizzled through her. She wanted to be closer, to meld with him. When he ended the kiss, his breath was as ragged as hers.

She tucked her head against his strong chest. "I was so nervous when I asked you to marry me. When you said we'd have a real marriage, I almost shouted for joy."

He caressed her arms. "I was kicking myself for not having the nerve to propose when you received that letter. But, here I am living in your boardinghouse with not much savings and my mother's care to oversee. I definitely didn't feel worthy."

"You are the most wonderful man."

"Now, though, I'm hoping we can turn in for our wedding night, my love. I'll wait in the other room if you want me to so you can get ready in private."

"I don't want to be apart from you unless I have to be."

"At least for the next fifty or sixty years, I'm yours."

"Barely long enough, my love."

98

Epilogue

Eighteen months later.

Merry cradled baby George. "Lucky we built an extra room for us when we added Ma's. Calvin's too old to share a room with babies."

Standing near the bed, Blake cradled baby Murphy. "Having twins is very efficient, my love, but I wasn't certain I'd survive their arrival. Are you certain you're all right?"

"Yes, I am now they're here and I won't have to waddle when I walk or feel like an elephant. Having twins will make our lives busier than we ever dreamed but they're so precious."

Ma took charge of Murphy. "Everyone out so Merry can rest. Blake, you go rest up, too. You look like a horse stomped you."

"Thank you, Ma. Actually, I feel like I'm walking on clouds. I'm not abandoning you to look after the children when you were up all night being midwife for Dr. Bushnell."

Calvin peered at little George. "They sure are red and wrinkled. Never mind, I'll take Abigail and Tammie to our tree house. I promise I'll watch 'em real good so you can nap."

Blake patted the boy's back. "Thanks, son. I know I can depend on you."

Calvin ushered Abigail and Tammie out of the room. Ma laid the babies in their cradles. She brought a damp cloth for Merry to use on her face.

Blake took charge of smoothing the wet cloth across Merry's face and then her arms and hands. When he finished, he leaned down to kiss Merry. "Don't forget how much I love you. Have sweet dreams of me while you sleep."

"My good dreams are always of you, dear. Stay here with me?

You can nap beside me." She patted the bed.

He glanced at his mother. "If General Grandma will allow me." He tentatively stretched out beside her, his feet sticking off the end of the bed several inches.

Ma shook her finger at him. "Don't you dare wiggle, Blake Woolf. Merry needs a lot of rest."

He raised his hand. "Solemn vow, Ma. I'll be still as a statue."

"See that you are. You'll have to give our little mother the babies as soon as they're hungry."

"I can do that. You know, I remember how to change diapers."

"Yes, you've had practice. I'll toddle off to bed then and leave you in charge of the babies and their mother."

When her mother-in-law had gone, Merry rested her head against her husband's arm. "Thank you for staying with me. I'm really tired, but I need you here."

"I'll try always to be available whenever you wish, my lady love. Go to sleep and I'll stay beside you."

She turned on her side and rested her hand on his broad chest. "Forever, I hope."

Gently, he kissed her forehead and held her close. "Count on me, my love. You can count on me."

About Caroline Clemmons

Through a crazy twist of fate, Caroline Clemmons was born in town instead of on a Texas ranch. To compensate for this illogical error, she writes about handsome cowboys, feisty ranch women, and scheming villains in a tiny office her family calls her pink cave. She and her Hero live in North Central Texas cowboy country where they ride herd on their three rescued indoor cats and dog as well as providing nourishment outdoors for squirrels, birds, and a collection of wild critters who stop by to visit.

The books she creates in her pink cave have made her a bestselling western author who has won awards. She writes both sweet and sensual romances about the West, both historical and contemporary as well as time travel and mystery. Her series include the Kincaids, McClintocks, Stone Mountain Texas, Bride Brigade, Texas Time Travel, Texas Caprock Tales, Pearson Grove, and Loving A Rancher as well as numerous single titles and contributions to multi-author sets including Pinkerton Matchmaker, Proxy Brides, Widows of Wildcat Ridge, and Bachelors and Babies.

When she's not writing, she loves spending time with her family, reading books written by her friends, eating out, browsing antique malls, checking Facebook, and taking the occasional nap. Find her on her **blog**, **website**, **Facebook**, **Twitter**, **Goodreads**, **Google+**, and **Pinterest**.

Join her and other readers at **Caroline's Cuties**, a Facebook readers group for special excerpts, exchanging ideas, contests, giveaways, recipes, and talking to like-minded people about books at **https://www.facebook.com/groups/277082053015947/**

Click on her **Amazon Author Page** for a complete list of her books and *follow* her there.

Follow her on **BookBub.**

To stay up-to-date with her releases and contests, subscribe to Caroline's newsletter **here** and receive a FREE novella of HAPPY IS THE BRIDE, a humorous historical wedding disaster that ends happily—but you knew it would, didn't you?

A Family For Polly
By
Jacquie Rogers

A FAMILY FOR POLLY

Chapter One

Mockingbird Flats, Texas, 1878

Polly Friday Bird snapped the tablecloth crisply over the makeshift wooden table while her sister Merry directed two men carrying benches. Polly wasn't so sure she wanted to meet the orphan train and help with recording which children were picked by local couples. Actually, she was very sure—she didn't want to do it at all. The very thought of the orphan train put a lump in her throat.

As Merry sat on the bench and took out the list of children and a pencil, Polly said, "I remember when we stood on the platform waiting for someone to pick us. Dread weighed down my insides as if I'd swallowed a cannonball."

Her sister half smiled and half grimaced. "I'd so hoped for a wonderful family that day. The Birds weren't it—but you were. I'll always be honored to call you my sister."

The train whistle blew and Polly heard the hiss of steam from the slowing train. "Yes, at least we have each other, and our brothers, too. Bart and Newt saved my behind from a lickin' more than once. Then again, I hated to see our brothers have to work as hard as they did, and the whippings."

She closed her eyes and willed the memories to go away. "I still remember putting horse liniment on the welts on their backs. None of us could get out of Nebraska fast enough, but I sure wish they'd come to Texas with us instead of heading to Colorado."

Merry nodded, an unfallen tear in her eye. "We'll see them again someday. I hope they've found their riches already."

Polly knew her sister was right to volunteer them both to assist with placing the orphans, painful as it might be. If the two of them helped, maybe they could find some way to prevent dreadful people from adopting any children. Mr. and Mrs. Bird, the couple who'd

103

adopted her and Merry along with Bartholomew and Newton, had been horrible and the Children's Society should have rejected them outright. The Birds had worked her and her adopted siblings until their hands bled and they'd collapsed from fatigue, only to be rousted out of bed at dawn the next day for even more backbreaking work.

Neither she nor her adopted siblings had been too sorrowful when the Birds passed on from eating a rhubarb pie that had accidentally included some of the poisonous leaves. Fortunately for Polly and her sister and brothers, the Birds had bought the pies at a church social and devoured them without sharing. Later, the young woman who'd donated the pie realized what must have happened and confessed, or Polly and Merry most certainly would've been blamed for the deaths.

Polly's thoughts returned to the job at hand when the Children's Society matron herded the orphans onto the platform and lined them up. Various couples, all of whom were good citizens, chose children, and Merry recorded them as Polly repeated the children's names. As always, there were some stragglers—those who weren't as pretty or perfect. Her heart went out to those children most of all.

"You see the last five, Merry? I don't want these orphans to wake up every morning wishing they'd perished on the streets of New York City, and go to bed wondering how they could do themselves in—anything to end it all."

Apparently that wouldn't happen to all of them because Merry wrote her own name beside the names of three of the children—a little girl with a limp named Abigail, the toddler that Abigail tended named Tamara, and then Calvin, a defiant boy of nine who'd most certainly have faced adversity had Merry not picked him.

Even so, Polly worried that Merry had overstepped. Merry assured her otherwise but she wasn't nearly as positive of a happy outcome. Still, she loved the idea of children in the house—they had plenty of room at the Mockingbird Flats Boardinghouse and a huge yard, an ideal place for the youngsters to run and play.

Then the last two children caught her eye—Noah, a strong boy, ten years old, whose eyes constantly scanned the crowd, and a waif-like girl named Evelyn who seemed glued to Noah's side.

"Next to last is this young fellow," the matron announced as she

104

pressed his shoulder to get him to step forward. "He's mute but generally biddable and stays out of trouble. He's strong enough to help on a farm or in a store."

Polly knew that if Noah grew into his ears and feet, he'd be a brawny fellow, and was at terrible risk to be put to hard labor. No one would want the scrawny girl, and Polly shuddered to think what atrocities could lie in wait for her.

She hurried to the two children. Evelyn clutched Noah's hand for dear life and pursed her lips, but she didn't cry. The matron nodded, so Polly said, "Evelyn, Noah, I'd like you to come live with me. Both of you. Would you like that?"

Noah studied her for a moment with a fretful frown then gestured to the girl, who slowly nodded.

"He wants to know if you promise to always take care of me...us?"

"I certainly will, and I also promise to make us all a family, complete with home and trust." Trust had been a hard quality for Polly to learn and she suspected Noah and Evelyn would have the same difficulty.

Noah pointed to his mouth.

"With food every day?" Evelyn asked.

"Three times a day. And snacks."

Evelyn squeezed Noah's hand. "And a warm place to sleep?"

"We have several quilts and you'll each have a feather mattress in a cozy room."

"Noah don't talk, but you can tell me and I'll tell you what his hand signals mean."

"That's perfectly fine. Actions speak louder than words, anyway. I just want the both of you to have a happy home, and I'd like that home to be with me."

"Then call me Evie, not Evelyn. Only the matron calls me Evelyn."

"Very well, I like that name." Polly smiled and motioned for them to follow her, which they did, and then she asked them to sit beside Merry's newly adopted children until the proceedings were over. After dodging the matron and speaking briefly with Reverend

Zebediah Jones then giving him the list of adoptive parents and their chosen children, she and Merry took their new families and discreetly left the church for home.

With children, it really would be a home.

* * *

The first few days, Noah and Evie—as she insisted to be called—were on their best behavior, other than a few missing dinner rolls and a missing plate of cheese. Polly couldn't get too bothered about that because she knew the filching would stop once the children became confident they'd always have three meals a day. Evie had caught some sort of stomach bug so had been sick on and off, but it didn't seem to slow her down much.

Polly was thankful for their compliance because she needed some time to get in the swing of being a mother. Besides, she had decided to move her family upstairs to the third-floor suite since the seven of them had been too crowded in the owner's suite on the ground floor. It didn't have a kitchen but then she didn't need one, and it did have two small bedrooms, a sitting room, and a washroom.

"Noah, will you be all right sleeping in a room by yourself?"

He shot her a scowl, threw his bag over his shoulder, and disappeared into his new bedroom.

Polly followed him. "Let me know how you'd like to redecorate the room. I'm of a mind that pink flowered wallpaper isn't your first choice."

Noah shrugged and proceeded to put his meager belongings in the trunk at the foot of the bed. Merry had taken her three children shopping, but because of Evie's continual stomach ailments, Polly hadn't been able to buy the things her two needed. Luckily, Merry had purchased a few things to tide them over until Evie felt more the thing.

The boy hadn't uttered a word since Polly had first seen him, and she had wracked her brain thinking of how she could get him to speak, if he even could. Maybe his vocal chords had been damaged and he was physically unable. Either way, she intended to take him to the doctor for a professional opinion and hopefully some advice.

But in the short term, his lack of speech didn't worry her as much as Evie's health. The little girl couldn't keep food down and had other

106

digestive disruptions as well, which embarrassed the poor girl to no end. On several occasions, Noah had tried to prevent Polly from caring for Evie by standing between them while Evie cleaned up her own messes. After two days, Noah began to understand that Polly wanted to make Evie more comfortable, not punish her, although he was still a mite skeptical.

When Polly returned to her own bedroom that she shared with Evie, she found the girl quickly cleaning up after yet another bout of vomiting.

Polly grabbed a towel. "I'll help you, Evie."

Noah pushed his way past her to shield his sister, and Polly wondered again what wrath Evie's illness had brought upon her before. Noah, no matter his other faults, was a loyal and honorable boy, defending his new sister as best he could.

"Noah, she isn't in trouble and won't be punished—I do realize she's ill. As soon as the doctor gets back to Mockingbird Flats, I'll make an appointment for her and maybe he can make her better."

Noah did relax his shoulders some, which made Polly happy.

She handed him a bowl. "Would you please fetch some warm water from the stove reservoir downstairs?"

He took the bowl but seemed torn about whether to leave Polly alone with Evie, or to get the water with which to wash her.

Polly wiped Evie's face with a handkerchief. "Would you like to lie down? Or sit in the chair?"

"I'll sit but I still need a bucket if you have one." Evie turned to Noah. "It's all right for you to get the water. I'll be fine with Miss Polly."

Noah studied them both, and must have been satisfied for he took the bowl and headed downstairs.

Polly straightened Evie's collar and brushed the girl's wispy light brown hair away from her cheeks. "Best get used to calling me *Mama*, or if you're not comfortable with that, then *Mama Polly*."

"I'll remember. But I ain't never had no mama before that I know of."

"And Noah?"

"Ain't sayin'."

107

Polly smiled to reassure the girl, and stood as Noah brought the warm water in and put it on the night stand. "We'll get you washed up and then if you're feeling better, we'll take a trip to the dress shop." She turned to Noah. "You're welcome to come along with us, and after we get some clothes for Evie, we'll go to the mercantile and buy you some shirts and britches. Looks like you both could use a new pair of shoes, too."

Later that afternoon, Evie finally felt better so Polly took the two children downtown to shop. Noah looked miserably uncomfortable in the dress shop but refused to leave his sister. Evie, however, was delighted to pick out materials for two new dresses.

On the way to the mercantile, Noah bumped into her and threw her off her stride. Then he moved to the other side of Evie. Polly saw him stash something in his jacket pocket. She smiled, remembering her own time on the back alleys of New York.

"I do believe we'll pass right by the confectionery," she told the children. "How would you like some candy?"

"Oh, yes!" Evie squealed.

But Noah just scuffed his new shoes on the boardwalk.

Polly maneuvered so that she was again walking beside him, then nudged him and lifted her coin purse out of his pocket.

She winked at him as she stashed the coin purse back into her reticule. "It's easier to buy candy when you have the money."

108

Chapter Two

One month later

When the going gets tough, the tough go to the candy store.

Polly Friday Bird sat on a stool at the counter of Bea's Confectionery and, without making eye contact with a soul lest they see how upset she was, stirred her tea with a peppermint stick. Her sister Merry, also upset, had gone to the dressmaker's shop but Polly had no desire to go with her even though she loved buying new clothes, especially for the children.

Growing up, she and Merry had worn ill-fitting dresses cut from their adoptive mother's tattered skirts, so both sisters delighted in dressing well now. Now that they'd each adopted children, they shared a desire to make sure the children wore decent clothing in styles and colors they liked. Still, Polly had other even more important problems to ponder.

A man came in and sat on the stool beside her. "Howdy, miss. Nice morning, isn't it?" She didn't look at him, but he smelled of bay rum and leather.

When she did glance up, perturbed that he'd interrupted her thoughts, she forced a smile. "Good morning." Once she got a good look, the smile came easy even with all her woes.

His handsome features held her gaze for longer than she'd intended. He was well-dressed in a gray sack suit laden with trail dust—no doubt he'd just disembarked from the stagecoach. His slightly long dark hair brushed his starched collar, and his broad shoulders would attract any woman whose blood still ran warm. Even so, it was his deep blue eyes that captured her gaze until she could manage to get back to concentrating on her hot tea.

But *good* morning? Hardly. The morning had been a trial. First, she couldn't interpret Noah's hand gestures in his silent plea for whatever it was he wanted, and while she concentrated on that, little Evie had barfed pancakes all over the kitchen table, two of the chairs,

109

and the floor. Once Polly had cleaned the kitchen and managed to find something that Noah would eat and Evie might keep down, Merry had announced that she had a visitor in the lobby.

Polly removed the peppermint stick from her tea cup and licked it off before she put it on the saucer, all the while wishing that instead of receiving the visitor, she'd gone straight upstairs and back to bed.

Mr. Ecclestone of the Children's Society had come to take Noah and Evie, and Merry's children, too, for the rules stated that all adoptive parents must be legally wed. If Polly and her sister didn't come up with a solution by the end of the week, he'd have no recourse but to remove all five children from their home.

The very thought broke Polly's heart.

"Looks like you've been here before." He scanned the candies in the display. "What fine morsel of delight should I order?"

Before Polly had a chance to answer, the owner came from the back and stepped up to the counter.

"Why, Ford Daily, is it you?" She grinned from ear to ear.

"It's me, all right." His voice rumbled low and pure, like warm maple syrup.

"What brings you to Mockingbird Flats?"

"You, my cute little neighbor girl."

"Your eyesight must be failing in your old age." Bea giggled. "I'm neither cute nor little, and I've grown up some since you last saw me." She opened the case, scooped some taffy onto a plate, and placed it in front of him. "I'll fetch you some coffee. How'd you know I was here?"

"Grandpa wrote me that you'd moved to town and started a candy store."

She slid a cup of coffee over the counter to him. "Are you back in Texas for good?"

"Yep. I'm officially graduated from Cornell and ready to doctor your animals."

"Don't have any."

He shrugged. "And ask you to marry me."

"That was quick." She reached over the counter and pinched his cheek. "I might even have thought about it if I wasn't already married."

"You're married?" He sounded aghast and disappointed.

"Just last week." Bea cocked her head at Polly. "Polly and her sister Merry were there."

Polly smiled shyly. "It was a beautiful wedding."

"Well, drat." Ford tapped his hat on his knee. "I really did come here to propose. Grandpa's being stubborn about deeding the ranch to me. Says since I'm the last Daily, he wants to see an heir before he pushes up daisies."

"Can't help you," Bea said. "Anyway, you have a bit of time. A fellow can't get much healthier than your grandpa—he's made of hearty stock."

"I know, but he's got a bur under his saddle. Told me not to come back without a bride. Problem is, I bought a herd and don't have anywhere to put them. Grandpa told me not to bring the cattle there unless I brought a wife, too."

"He can't mean that." To Polly, Bea said, "Can I get you anything else?"

Polly sipped her minty tea. "I'd like a bag of peppermint sticks and one husband, please." She turned to Ford. "I have to be married by the end of the week or they'll take my children."

Ford raised an eyebrow. "Didn't you get that in the wrong order? Folks generally get married before they have babies."

"They're not babies."

He eyed her a moment. "Why would anyone take your children?"

"Merry came in earlier so I know about the Children's Society lawyer," Bea said to Polly. Then she turned to Ford. "Merry and Polly adopted several youngsters from the orphan train. None of the children stood a chance of getting a decent home, but they're doing well now."

"Sounds like a batch of lucky young'uns to me," Ford said.

Polly thought it was the other way around—Noah and Evie were blessings to her. "We're doing well. I just want what's best for them."

Bea waited on another customer then came back. "I'm dreadful sorry you won't be able to keep the orphans. Noah and Evie seem so happy now—they act much more like normal children than when they arrived. I remember how scared they were the first time you brought them in."

Polly turned to Ford, who seemed more amused than worried. "I'm serious. You need a wife and I need a husband. We can get copies of the marriage certificate and once your grandfather and the Children's Society lawyer are satisfied, we can get an annulment."

"Not a bad idea," Bea said. "You're two good people who can help each other out." She looked at Ford, then at Polly. "Why not?"

That's when the handsome Ford Daily turned to Polly and said, "Would you marry me, Polly? That *is* your name, right?"

Her breath caught, for he affected her like no other man ever had, and she'd turned down her share of suitors. Another time, another situation, and Polly might've lost her heart to this man, but she was entering a business arrangement. She had to remember that. "I accept, and my full name is Polly Friday Bird."

"Manford Daily, but everyone calls me Ford." He raised an eyebrow. "Friday? That's a strange middle name."

"It was the surname given to me at the orphanage. I was found on a Friday."

"You were an orphan?"

"Yes, and I know how dreadfully hard it can be for a child to grow up in harsh circumstances—that's why I simply can't bear to see Noah and Evie put to such a trial."

"Well then, I assume you know a preacher?"

"That would be Reverend Zebediah Jones. I can contact him forthwith."

"I'll be at the church with wedding treats as soon as you schedule a ceremony," Bea said. "Ford, you can use my husband as a best man. And Polly, if Merry's not there, I can stand up with you."

"When would be a good time?" Ford asked.

"The sooner, the better." Polly had seen the reverend earlier when she was utterly beside herself so she reckoned he was still in the rectory. "I can go make arrangements now, if you're of a mind."

"And this will help your children?"

"It will *save* my children."

* * *

Noah held his hands out flat and circled both forefingers.

"We're in trouble?" Evie asked.

He shook his head then pointed to Polly's side of the bed.

"Polly's in trouble?"

He nodded. He'd come to trust his new mother, and like her, too. Even more than like, maybe, and he didn't want to see her in trouble because she'd given him and Evie a home. He pointed to Evie, then himself, and then walked his right-hand fingers across his left palm.

"We're leaving?" Evie's eyes grew big. "Where would we go?"

He shrugged. Then pretended to filch from the pocket of her new dress.

"I know we can get along—we did when we lived in Master Geldart's protection."

Noah scowled.

"Yeah, some protection." Evie's shoulders sagged. "When do we leave?"

He pointed to her trunk, then slipped the pillow out of its case and handed the pillowcase to her.

"I'll gather my things now." When he picked up his own bag, she said, "I'll hurry."

Once they got downstairs, they stashed their bags outside in the bushes on the far side of the yard and came back in the house and found Aunt Merry.

As he'd instructed, Evie asked, "Is it all right if we go outside and play?"

"Sure." Aunt Merry rocked the toddler who slept in her arms. "Would you like to take some cookies with you? Mrs. Koch just made some oatmeal raisin."

Evie and Noah both nodded. He'd sorely miss Mrs. Koch's cookies—and all the food. Neither he nor Evie had ever eaten food so tasty or so plentiful as at the Mockingbird Flats Boardinghouse. Even more than the food, he'd miss the friendly talk and occasional joshing.

In Master Geldart's alley, the kid who ate the fastest got the most, even if the food was full of dirt and bugs, and likely rancid, too. The meals at the orphanage had been eaten in silence, and the food all

113

tasted the same, no matter whether meat or vegetable. Sometimes he couldn't tell the difference.

"Tell Mrs. Koch that you can have two cookies each," Aunt Merry said. "If you see Calvin, tell him we're having fried chicken for supper and he's guaranteed a drumstick." She winked. "That way, he'll be sure to show up on time."

Calvin was another orphan boy. Aunt Merry had adopted him, the baby she was holding, and a girl named Abigail. Noah wondered where Abbie had gotten herself off to, for she seldom ever left the little one.

Noah waved good-bye and smiled, although he didn't feel like smiling, for he had a fondness for her, the boardinghouse, the residents, and most especially Mama Polly. He really hated to go and felt a pang of guilt for asking Mrs. Koch for the cookies even though Aunt Merry said they could have them. Evie must have felt the same, for once they ran into the yard and grabbed their bags from the bushes, a tear trailed down her cheek.

He pointed at himself, so that she knew he felt the same. They took off at a brisk pace. He led his sister to the part of town where the saloons were, for he knew Mama Polly would never go there. He wandered nonchalantly, keeping close track of Evie lest she get snatched away, while looking for a vehicle that would take them away from Mockingbird Flats.

"I hope Mama Polly doesn't come looking for us too soon," Evie said.

She echoed his own thoughts. Mama Polly would try to keep them, but the orphan people would take him and Evie anyway and that would hurt her. It was better if he and Evie left.

He and Evie headed to a barrel to hide behind, but Deputy Barnell, who lived at the boardinghouse, was escorting a handcuffed prisoner down the boardwalk and saw them before they could get there. The deputy was an agreeable fellow and all the orphans liked him, but he'd tell Mama Polly where they were.

"What're you doing in this part of town?" he called to them. "You young'uns best get yourselves home right now."

"Yes, sir!" Evie called.

114

Noah pulled her along with him as if they were doing exactly as the deputy had told them to do, but when he and the prisoner rounded the corner, Noah and Evie scrambled back to where they were before—it was the best vantage point to see all the comings and goings on the two main streets.

They waited for another several minutes. No one paid attention to them except for a drunk man who asked them for a bottle of whiskey. Noah shrugged and showed the man empty hands.

"Too scared to talk, eh?" the drunk said.

Evie jammed her hands on her bony little hips. "Noah ain't scared of nothin' and neither am I."

Noah tugged on Evie's sleeve and led her across the street where they wouldn't be bothered while waiting for a good opportunity to catch a ride out of town. Didn't anyone in this part of town use a wagon? Lots of folks had wagons where the mercantile stores and the like were, but in the saloon and brothel section, men either walked or rode horses.

Finally, a man with a wagon pulled to a stop in front of the Red Dog Saloon. He tongued his soggy cigar from one side of his mouth to the other and adjusted his sweaty dirt-caked derby. Then he hopped off the wagon, walked to the back of the bed, and flipped back a heavy blanket to reveal a load of barrels. He pulled out a couple of planks that he used for a ramp, and then, with a grunt and a groan, the fellow managed to get one barrel tipped and rolled down to the road.

Noah knew the barrels had to hold either whiskey or beer, but he'd bet it was whiskey. There'd be enough room in the wagon for himself and Evie. All he had to do was wait and see if the driver would unload more, or all of the barrels. Noah elbowed Evie and she nodded.

They waited and waited. What seemed like forever later, the man came back and flipped the cover back over the remaining barrels. Then he gawked around a bit, lit another cigar, and finally climbed back up to the driver's seat. But he didn't flick the reins. Noah wondered why he was dilly-dallying so.

A huge lady whose bosom nearly busted out of her corset walked by Noah and Evie. Noah got in step with her, behind and to her left, so she wouldn't notice. Evie did the same. The lady walked right by the wagon, and quick as a whistle, Noah sneaked onto the wagon. He reached out and pulled Evie on with him. Then they wiggled around so the barrels and blankets would hide them from everyone.

Chapter Three

After Polly left to make arrangements to be married, Ford munched on the taffy and wondered what on earth he'd gotten himself into. Miss Bird was a mighty comely lass—blond hair and shapely figure that made him ache to put his hands around her small waist. But what man in his right mind would marry a woman he'd never even seen before?

He'd come to Mockingbird Flats to marry Bea. She'd always been game for whatever he suggested, with few exceptions—not because he'd suggested them, but on account of she was the most daring gal he'd ever met.

In fact, he had a hard time picturing her being happy while stuck in a confectionery all day. Even so, she did look happy and seemed quite taken with her new husband. He hoped that continued for he wished her all the best.

But Miss Polly Friday Bird... that woman intrigued him in more ways the one. In more ways than she should. He'd been drawn to her right off the bat as she sat at the candy counter stirring her tea with a peppermint stick. She'd looked so alone and dejected. And beautiful. He had a strong notion to protect her and make everything right for her.

Maybe he was doing exactly that—all except for the big hug, which he still wouldn't mind.

Bea came back and tapped her knuckles on the counter to get his attention. "So what do you think of Polly?"

He wasn't about to tell Bea what he'd been thinking. "She seems like a nice lady who wants to do right by the orphans she adopted."

"She's the genuine article—sweet as they come, smart as a whip, and not bad looking, either. Several of the gents around here have tried to court her, but she wasn't interested in any of them."

"Even to keep her children?"

"My guess is she likely was considering marrying one of them, but she wouldn't do that except as a last resort because they'd consider it a real marriage. With you, it satisfies her need for a husband and your need for a wife. You'll go away and she won't have to worry about being married to a man she doesn't love."

"Love? So Miss Bird's a romantic." She was sounding better all the time.

"Very much so," Bea said. "And picky when it comes to men."

"What if I don't leave?"

"Of course you'll go. You've spent your whole life planning how you'll improve the ranch once it's yours."

"I could set up a veterinarian office here in Mockingbird Flats."

"That would cheer up your grandpa, all right. He's never made it a secret that your main job in life is producing little Dailys, and he wants them born on his ranch."

"I know, I've heard it a thousand times—the land is in your blood. Well, it's in mine but he's making other occupations look mighty blasted good."

"Are you planning to take Polly to the ranch?"

Ford leaned on his elbows and finger-combed the hair on the back of his head. "She doesn't seem like she wants to go anywhere. And I don't even know her."

"Well, I know her, and she's a fine lady. So don't you go taking advantage."

"Dadburn it, Bea—pardon my French—you know I wouldn't do any such thing." But he'd thought of it right off, and this was one of those times he wished he weren't so damnably honorable.

"Where are you staying?"

"You tell me. Is there a hotel?"

"Was. Now it's the Mockingbird Flats Boardinghouse."

"I'll get a room there if they have a vacancy. Where is it?"

Bea gave him directions while Ford sneaked a fifty-cent piece under his plate, for she'd refused to let him pay for his candy and coffee.

"I'll be back by once I find out when and where the wedding is."

"Or I can let Polly know where you are and she can tell you."

"That'd work." He put on his hat and left.

First stop—the livery. He didn't see any horses worth buying so he rented a bay gelding. The horse didn't have all that good of conformation but he looked like he had heart. Ford mounted the gelding and rode to the stage stop, where he picked up his valise and made arrangements for his trunk to be delivered to the boardinghouse. He briefly considered having it sent ahead to the ranch, but decided he wanted to arrive at the ranch complete with bride, trunk, and anything she might bring.

All he had to do was convince Polly to go with him. He wouldn't force her to stay at the ranch, although if he were in a room full of women, he'd have picked her first go. But he did need for her to present herself to his grandpa as his wife. Once the deed was signed over, then she could do as she wished.

He hoped she would wish to stay with him, but she didn't send him any sign of interest whatsoever.

Not even one flirty glance.

Mockingbird Flats Boardinghouse was only a block from Main Street and not far from the livery, but Ford rode there anyway because he wanted to see if the rental horse had a decent gait. The boardinghouse loomed large, even on a spacious lot. His first impression was a positive one—the building's white trim accented the fresh yellow paint, and the sign with a carving of a mockingbird welcomed one and all.

The interior wasn't fancy but well-kept. He strode to the registration desk, where a pretty lady clerk with light brown hair and a ready smile met him. She was quite tall and dressed well for a clerk. Ford decided Mockingbird Flats had a good share of the beautiful women in Texas.

"How may I help you, sir?"

"Looking for a room, please."

"We have a one-week minimum stay."

"That's fine."

"I'm afraid the only room we have available is a suite on the third floor."

"How much?"

She told him, and the price was a bit stiff for him since he still had to live on his education stipend his grandpa had given him until he established his business, but he didn't have much choice.

"You have a wash room, a sitting room, and two bedrooms. You'll have to fetch your own water. We serve two full meals a day except Sunday. If you're not here at mealtime, you'll have to fend for yourself. Sheets are changed once a week." She handed him a key.

"Thank you, miss."

Two kids nearly tripped him on the stairs—a squealing little girl was chasing a slightly older boy up one more flight of stairs and into the room opposite his. Looked as if they were having a good time.

That's what childhood was for.

Ford entered the suite, surprised at how spacious and homey it was. The couch in the sitting room looked comfortable, as did the overstuffed chair. In the corner was a secretary and chair, along with an empty bookshelf.

He shrugged off his jacket, brushed the dust from it and his hat, then hung them on hooks beside the armoire. The rest of his settling in would have to wait on account of his stomach growled for food—the taffy had been tasty but he hadn't eaten a decent meal since he'd left Ithaca, New York. A big beef steak and a pile of mashed potatoes floating in gravy would hit the spot.

A man shouldn't get married on an empty stomach.

Someone knocked on the door and he answered it. The woman who'd rented the room to him stood there holding a bucket of water and a wicker basket.

"I thought you might like some wash water to freshen up. We don't normally bring water but bein's this is your first day and since I was coming up anyway to bring you some food—"

"Food?" That got his attention. He took the bucket from her and poured it into the ewer on the nightstand. "I was just regretting that I'd checked in after mealtime."

"I brought some roast beef, bread and butter, and a bowl of potatoes and gravy."

"I swear, you must've come straight from heaven, for I'm famished." He took the basket and put it on the trunk. "I'll bring the dishes down directly."

"Thanks, I'll leave you be. I hope the children haven't disturbed you."

"Not at all." He studied her features. The youngsters didn't resemble her at all. "Are they yours?"

"No, they're my sister's. They live in the suite across the hall, but I'm watching them today and they were supposed to stay downstairs."

"Aw, you know how kids are." He knew how he'd been—tearing around the countryside with Bea and his other friends, always finding some trouble to get into and sometimes even out of.

"I'll fetch them and they won't bother you."

Ford would've protested but that roast beef smelled mighty good. "Much obliged, but they aren't bothering me."

"All the same." She bobbed her head sort of like an old-fashioned curtsy. "I'll be going now."

Ford shut the door and went straight to the food basket. It'd been a crazy day, but a little food ought to help.

*   *   *

After making arrangements with the reverend, Polly hurried home to tell her sister the news. Normally, a wedding would be good news, but in this case it was just plain news. But she'd do anything, including marrying a complete stranger, to keep her children—not just for their sakes, but because she'd come to love them.

She went in the back way, pulled Merry into her suite, and shut the door to avert prying ears.

"What's got you in such a state?" Merry asked, rubbing her arm.

Polly felt a mite sorrowful for gripping her sister's arm so tightly. "I have an answer to my problem—I'm getting married today."

"Married? Who?" Merry tilted her head and her gaze nearly bore a hole through Polly. "Reggie Norris?"

Reggie was the town's blacksmith who'd courted Polly on occasion. She liked him well enough but certainly didn't love him and had turned down his offer of marriage a few months back.

"No, it's no one you know. He's a veterinarian named Ford Daily and he's in need of a wife. I'm in need of a husband so it seemed fortuitous that we met at Bea's Confectionery."

"Polly, you simply can't pick the first man you see and marry

121

him."

"But it will help us both. I say again—he needs to have a wife right away and I need a husband."

"So you're leaving? Where does he live?"

"Not leaving. He'll go to his ranch and show the marriage papers, and then his grandfather will sign over the deed. I'll get the Children's Society satisfied and after both those things are taken care of, we'll get an annulment."

"But Polly, what if he wants to keep you?"

"That won't happen because he knows I'm staying here with the children and he'll be riding out of town to his grandpa's ranch—he has to, for he has a herd on the way."

"You're not making any sense at all. Why does he have to be there for a herd to get there?"

"Because his grandpa won't let him move the herd there until he's married."

"Stop and think about this. Mr. Ecclestone could be here an entire week. What if your new husband rides out of town before then? Sounds like he very well might if he's in such a big hurry to be married."

"We haven't discussed this, but it's better than doing nothing." Polly held up two fingers squeezed together. "You're this close to losing your children, too. Do you have a better way to avert the disaster?"

"I'm thinking on it."

"Well, I'm doing something about it."

"Polly, you can't! What if he beats you, or robs you blind? You have no idea what kind of man he is."

"Bea grew up with him and she vouched for him. Anyway, it really doesn't matter—he has business to take care of so he'll be on his way out of town directly. After the ceremony, I'll have no association with him whatsoever. He's already agreed to an annulment."

Whether Merry agreed or not, Polly saw marrying Ford Daily as the only way to keep her children, and nothing mattered more.

Chapter Four

The stage company delivered Ford's trunk to his third floor room. Glad he hadn't had to lug it up three flights of stairs, he unpacked his clothes and firearms. He stowed the latter high in the armoire so the youngsters couldn't get to them, although he doubted they'd come into his rooms. Then he tested the bed and woke up an hour later. It'd take a while for him to catch up on his sleep after the grueling train trip, but the nap helped.

Next thing he had to do was get married. But he had no idea how to contact his future bride. He headed back to the confectionery hoping that Bea would know.

"Hi, Ford," Bea called from behind the counter. She made one last swipe with a towel and tossed it onto her shoulder. "Have a seat. We don't have any customers and my feet are killing me so I'll fetch us both a cup of coffee."

He sat at a table by the window in order to see if Miss Polly walked by. "Coffee sounds good."

In no more than a wink, Bea set two mugs on the table. "Sugar and cream?"

He stood and pulled out a chair for her. "Nope, this is fine. Take a load off your feet."

"We just made a batch of toffee. Want some?"

"Sounds good but I just ate. They serve great food at the boardinghouse."

She sank onto the chair. "I've heard that."

"Has Miss Polly been by?" Ford returned to his own seat. "She didn't ever say where we should meet."

"Sounds like you're all-fired anxious to get married."

He let out a deep breath. "My stomach doesn't much like the proposition even though I have to say that Miss Polly is easy on the eyes."

"She certainly is pretty, and I bet you're a mite on the anxious side, but knowing you, you're bound and determined to satisfy your grandpa."

That's what this mess was all about—his grandpa Moses Austin Daily. "Whatever the family patriarch wants, I'll do my level best to acquire, for even though he's being stubborn about the whole deal, the purebred Angus herd I bought will be the seed stock to ensure the future of the Rocking MAD. He doesn't seem to understand that I *am* working to continue his legacy."

People walked by the confectionery and peeked through the windows longingly. Ford almost felt guilty for not eating another piece of candy, but the fine roast beef dinner would be hard to top, even with sweets. And his stomach had enough to deal with.

Bea picked up her coffee mug with both hands, blew the steam off, and took a sip. "I bet his contrariness gets you hot under the collar."

"Naw. Grandpa Mo's set in his ways all right, but I can't be too irritated with him because his heart's in the right place."

Bea reached over the table and patted Ford's hand. "I'm sorry about your folks. Must've been hard being in New York when they passed."

Bea couldn't know the half of it. He'd wanted to be home to take care of his family when they were in need, and he'd felt guilty for carrying on with his studies at Cornell, but that's what his grandpa had wanted.

"Have you seen Miss Polly?"

"No, but I expect she'll be by directly. When Polly makes up her mind to do something, we all just stand back and watch." Bea grinned. "That woman is a force."

"A good force, I hope."

Bea's grin reflected the mischievous glint in her eye. "I expect you'll find out soon enough."

He spotted Miss Polly, pretty as spring's first bluebonnet, clutching her reticule in one hand and holding a parasol in the other, walking briskly toward Bea's candy store. "I expect you're right, as usual." He stood and opened the door for his bride. "Good afternoon, Miss Polly."

"I'm glad you're here—saves me from having to look for you." Miss Polly closed her parasol and hooked it over her arm, then entered the candy store. "I have all the particulars."

"Good." He pulled out a chair next to Bea. "Have a seat and you can tell me all about it."

She sat, and he went back to where he'd sat before.

"I talked to the reverend," she announced. "He's available at four o'clock. He'd like us to chat with him for a few minutes before he performs the ceremony."

"Sounds reasonable."

"You've changed clothes." She blushed, for he suspected she considered the remark inappropriate.

"Got ready for the wedding early. The roast beef dinner at the boardinghouse didn't hurt, either—really hit the spot."

"You ate at the boardinghouse?"

"Yes, a nice lady runs it. I checked in just after mealtime so she brought the food to my room."

She laughed. "One nice lady and one crabby lady."

"Crabby? I guess I didn't meet that one."

She pointed at herself. "Meet Polly Friday Bird, half-owner of Mockingbird Flats Boardinghouse. You chose a nice place to stay."

He was a mite taken aback, but on second thought, Miss Polly showed an enterprising nature. "The only place, according to Bea."

Bea blushed. "Well, there's another boardinghouse on the other side of town, but..."

"Not to worry," Miss Polly said to Bea. "We appreciate your referrals." She turned to Ford. "We'll be married in the church at four o'clock if you're still of a mind."

Ford took a long sip of his coffee. "I am."

"You sound as if you have reservations. Well, so do I. What we're about to do is neither sensible nor prudent, but it will solve huge problems for both of us."

Bea stood and picked up her cup. "Is your sister able to go?"

"No, Merry's watching the children. If you have the time, I'd be ever so grateful if you'd stand up with me."

"My pleasure."

"I have to go home and get ready, so I'll meet you at the church."

"We'll close early—I already told Steve we'd likely be needed sometime today. And since we'll be walking right by your place, we'll stop and pick you up at the boardinghouse in half an hour, give or take ten minutes."

"That would be fine." Miss Polly stood. "I'll see you then," she said as she went through the door.

Ford didn't understand the need. "I'm staying at the boardinghouse—I'll escort my bride."

"No, you won't," Bea said as she tidied the table. "It's bad luck for the groom to see the bride's wedding dress. It's bad enough you've seen her already today. You'll stay here and Steve will take you to the church." She headed to the kitchen.

But he hadn't even met Miss Polly before today. Their marriage would definitely have a wobbly beginning.

* * *

Polly rushed home to change clothes as quickly as possible. The boardinghouse cook, Elvira Koch, met her at the door.

"My goodness, you're in a hurry," she said to Polly.

"I'm solving problems. If the Children's Society wants me to be married, then I'll get married." She didn't hear any familiar giggles from the youngsters. "Where are the children?"

"Merry took them out to play. I think they met some other children and your sister wanted to get them acquainted before school started."

"Thank you for telling me." At least Polly didn't have to worry about Noah and Evie. "I'm going upstairs to dress and then I'll be on my way to the church. If my sister comes back soon, please let her know where I am, but I don't think it's a good idea for the children to be there."

As Polly climbed the stairs, she was glad she didn't have to explain things to Evie and Noah, for she had no idea how they'd react. They might be excited about the prospect of having a father even though they weren't actually getting one, and then they'd be disappointed. Or they might think of Ford as an intruder into their family even though she had no intention of him becoming the head of

126

household, but she felt confident Ford would never poke his nose in where he wasn't wanted. Her children only needed to know that she would do anything and everything in her power to make sure they were safe and loved.

Since Merry was gone, Polly didn't have anyone to help her dress. Washing up didn't take any time at all since the ewer already had water in it. Luckily, she was used to lacing her own corset, which she did, giving it an extra tug. The problem came with hairstyling at which Polly was hopelessly inept, but her sister could manage quite well. So Polly ran a brush through her hair and pinned it up as best she could, making sure no stray locks escaped.

After staring at her gowns, all of which were relatively new, she decided to wear her newest dress—a fairy tale pink long-tail bodice over a cream skirt. The bodice had front darts that emphasized her assets and the seamed back flared out with plenty of material to cover her bustle and still trail clear to the floor. It had little trimming and was the most daring of all her dresses. Besides, she hadn't worn it before.

Merry had talked her into purchasing a pink bonnet to match, for which Polly was grateful. Even though it wouldn't be a real marriage in God's eyes, it certainly was a legal one and she didn't want to look like a dowd.

And if the mirror didn't lie, she'd achieved her goal—all except for her pathetic hairdo, but the bonnet would cover most of it.

While she looked put-together on the outside, her innards were as mixed up as the cream she used to churn for hours on end to make butter. At least something good came out of all that cream, and she sincerely hoped her marriage to Ford would benefit both of them and her children.

"Are you ready, Polly?" Elvira called through the door. "Bea's here!"

Polly was dressed in her finest, but did that mean she was ready? She'd never be ready, but she had to soldier on for the children's sake. "I'll be out in a minute."

Polly gave her skirts one last tug, pinned on her bonnet, and checked the mirror to make sure she was presentable, then opened the door.

Bea looked quite pretty in her green Sunday dress. "Well, Polly, you certainly got ready in a hurry and you look absolutely ravishing. Ford's eyes will pop plumb out the sockets when he sees his beautiful bride."

"I don't know about that, but we'd better get going lest we be late." Polly led the way down the three flights of stairs.

"I sent Steve and Ford to the florist shop," Bea said as they walked down the path that led to the street. "There won't be much of a selection but at least you'll have a bridal bouquet."

"Thanks, flowers are nice—but not really necessary. We'll be saying our vows in private, signing the papers, and that's that. No one will know other than Mr. Ecclestone and Ford's grandfather. Once my children are truly mine, and Ford's grandfather signs the deed over, then we'll get an annulment and we'll both be free to marry whomever we please."

They turned onto Main Street. As they walked in front of the mercantile, Jane Dorchester greeted them.

"Shopping today?" she asked.

"No," Bea said. "Polly's getting married."

Polly could've stuffed her reticule in Bea's mouth.

Jane put down the tools she'd been arranging and smiled. "Married? Oh my, this is quite sudden." She gazed at Polly's midriff.

Lavinia Zimmerman, wife of the bank teller, and her son came out of the mercantile, each holding a parcel. "Polly, did I hear right? You're getting married?"

"Yes, but..."

"How wonderful—congratulations!" Lavinia grabbed her newly adopted son's hand. "I can hardly wait to tell Dennis. We'll see you at the church."

"But..." There was no use for Polly to say anything else because Lavinia had already headed down the street toward the bank.

"Looks like you'll be having a few guests," Bea said.

Polly groaned and picked up the pace. "We have to get to the church before they do. I don't want Ford thinking I invited half the town to a wedding that unites us in name only."

128

"Four people isn't half the town. But then you know how it is in Mockingbird Flats—any excuse for a party."

Chapter Five

"We're not having a party." The last thing Polly wanted was for anyone to make a commotion about this wedding, especially when the marriage would be over in a few short weeks if all went well. In fact, she was hoping to keep the whole arrangement quiet, for a big wedding to-do would make explaining why she wasn't married after a short while all that much harder. "The whole ceremony will be over in fifteen minutes and after that I have work to do—I haven't even done my morning chores yet."

"Fifteen minutes? I bet it'll take you fifteen minutes to get through the front door. And another hour after for visiting if you're lucky," Bea said, huffing to keep up with Polly's brisk pace. "You know very well that the ladies will be excited to have something new to talk about, and every single one of them will want to meet Ford."

Bea was right, but Polly still had hopes of keeping the wedding as quiet as possible. "I don't want any of them to meet Ford."

As they passed by the fire station, Fiona Bushnell, the fire chief's wife, followed behind them saying, "I was in the florist shop a while ago and heard that you're getting married so I was on my way to the church. With such short notice, I didn't have a chance to make you a nice gift, but I ordered some apple turnovers from the bakery to be delivered."

Polly stopped and Bea had to take a few steps back to stay with her. Her throat tightened but she managed to say, "Thank you, Fiona. That was a lovely thing to do."

"Oh, and I invited Jessica. I hope you don't mind."

Polly certainly did mind but since Polly hadn't invited Fiona either, she could hardly say that she objected to Fiona inviting her sister-in-law, the town doctor's wife. "Of course not. That was very neighborly of you." She nearly choked on her words.

Jessica Bushnell hailed them with a wave. "I'm so happy for you, Polly!" She held up a basket. "Baby things. I've been saving them

130

for our town's next wedding. First baby can come anytime—the other ones take nine months." She giggled. "We won't mention how many first babies in this town were premature."

"Thank you, but I'm not in a family way."

The matronly lady winked. "You will be shortly, then."

Polly tugged on Bea's arm. "We best be on our way." She set off for the church once again, this time with several ladies and a few gentlemen following. So much for her secret marriage. With luck, Ford wouldn't be put off by the folderol and back out of their deal.

She cast a glance at Bea, who had the decency to look sheepish.

"I don't know where they got the idea that you're having a baby."

"How many people did you tell, for land's sake?"

"Only Jane Dorchester just now. Honest! I didn't tell anyone else."

Polly didn't want to upset her friend but this whole affair was turning into a fiasco—and all for a wedding to a man she didn't even know.

By the time they got to the church, several buggies were parked alongside and people were milling about. Polly stopped cold and Fiona bumped into her back.

"I'm so sorry. Are you all right? You look a mite stunned."

Considering her stomach had taken a swan dive when she'd seen all those people, no she wasn't all right. Not at all.

"I'm fine, just a bit nervous."

Fiona took Polly's hand. "Weren't we all. You'll be fine."

Jessica shouldered in between Bea and Fiona. "We're here with you to help—whatever you need, just ask."

What Polly needed was a whole lot less help and all these people to be gone, but she kept her counsel.

The banker's wife, Vallie Collins, rushed out of the church and headed straight for Polly. "We have the reception set up out back of the church, so we'll go there directly after the ceremony. You best come inside now—your groom's waiting and he seems a mite anxious—pacing and all." Since Vallie's husband was also mayor of Mockingbird Flats, Polly might as well have put out flyers announcing the wedding to every residence in town.

131

"That's perfectly natural," Jessica said. "My Eugene's knees were knocking together so hard that they sounded like a clogger was dancing on the altar."

For two cents, Polly would hightail it back home, but she couldn't, for the children were counting on her. They might not know it, but they'd shown no hope for the future when they'd first arrived, and the mere fact that they were learning to play said a lot about their chances of leading normal lives—even Noah, who still hadn't uttered a word.

With her children in mind, she straightened her shoulders and headed for the church door. This marriage would've been a lot easier to stomach if the townspeople were home or working like they were supposed to be. But easy or hard, Polly was determined to go through with the sham until her children's future was secure.

* * *

Ford waited with Steve in a little room off the side of the altar. Occasionally, he'd peek through a slit in the door as the people entered the sanctuary and seated themselves. Many carried gifts or flowers, and some brought food.

"The first five pews on both sides are plumb full, Steve," he grumbled. "I thought this would be a quick ceremony so we could sign the papers and tend to business."

"We just went through this last week. I wanted to get married at the courthouse but Bea wanted a church wedding, so I had to grit my teeth and keep remembering that it'd be over shortly, which it was. Relatively painless, actually, and the end benefit was worth all the trouble."

"Yeah, well I'm not going to get any 'end benefit.' Why'd she invite all these people?"

"Best ease up on Polly—she couldn't have." Steve sat on a wooden chair in the corner and rested his ankle on his knee. "She didn't have time. My guess is the florist spread the word. Myrtle's not known to keep a confidence more than ten minutes. And anyway, you know as well as I do that in a small town, your neighbor knows your business before you do."

"Yep. Same in Dailyville, but that doesn't ease my mind much."

"You can always jilt her at the altar."

Ford did feel like bolting, but he'd given his word. At that moment, it seemed like a hasty word.

"Can't do that to her. We only met today and we've talked for a short few minutes, but that was enough time for me to see that her intentions are honorable and she has a sincere soul."

"That pretty much describes our Polly. Everyone in Mockingbird Flats has taken a liking to her and her sister Merry. They bought the hotel and turned it into a boardinghouse—astute at business, they are, and always ready to help someone in need."

"Sounds as if you're talking about two angels." He clasped his hands behind him and walked the two steps across the room, then back.

"It does, but I'm sure they have their faults. We all do."

"They don't look alike at all." He ruffled his hair, then patted it down and took another tour around the room. What he needed was a good brisk ride with wind in his face and bugs in his teeth.

"They're adopted sisters, not blood sisters. Seems like that makes them closer for some reason."

Ford went back to the door and took another look into the sanctuary. "The place is nearly full now. I wish the preacher would get the show on the road."

"You might as well sit your sorry butt in that chair over there. This room isn't big enough for your infernal pacing."

The reverend called through the door. "The bride's here. Are you ready?"

"Ready as any man who's waiting at the gallows," Ford muttered.

"Join the club." Steve snorted as he stood. "Let's get you hitched up to the second prettiest girl in Mockingbird Flats."

Ford wasn't so sure about that—Bea was pretty, all right, but Polly... well, he had a hard time keeping the image of her sweet lips from his baser thoughts.

He opened the door when he heard piano music.

Mendelssohn's *Wedding March*.

* * *

Noah worried that all the jostling would make Evie sick. Just

133

about everything made her sick. Really, she was a lot of trouble but he'd always felt the need to protect her. They hadn't been captured by the Children's Society at the same time—they caught her first, and then him a month or so later.

He didn't only worry about the jostling. The tarp covering the load seemed to suck in the heat of the afternoon sun, and they'd already drunk all the water in the canteen he'd brought. He'd never been so hot in his life.

She motioned to him asking when they'd get off the wagon.

He walked his fingers across his palm indicating they'd sneak off when they got to some people—in a town. Only thing was, he worried there wouldn't be a town anytime soon. He could survive in a town but he didn't know a thing about the country and neither did Evie.

Evie took a coin purse out of her skirt pocket and handed it to him.

The coins came to several dollars, enough to buy some food for a week if they were careful. He raised an eyebrow and gazed at her.

She grinned and rubbed her thumb on her first and second fingers.

After a while, the driver hollered, "Whoa!" and the wagon stopped.

Noah peeked from under the tarp and saw several men around a campfire, and one walking toward the wagon.

"Did you make a good deal, Boss?" the man said.

"Fair to middlin'." The driver hopped off the wagon. "You unload the empty barrels. We have to refill tonight, for old Lucky bought two more barrels than I thought he would."

"You hungry? There's flapjacks on the griddle if you want some."

Noah heard the driver fiddling with the tarp ties. What should he and Evie do? He'd already planned how they were going to sneak off the wagon, but he didn't know what direction to go after that. Always in the city, they'd run off and mingle with the crowd. Except he didn't think there was a crowd within fifty miles.

He poked Evie and gave her the "run fast" signal.

The man flipped the tarp open.

Noah and Evie took off like a musket shot. One thing they knew

134

how to do was get away from mean grownups, and that worked whether they were in the alleys of New York or the hot Texas emptiness.

He grabbed Evie's arm and headed for a big pile of rocks. Only then did he realize he'd left the bag of food they'd pilfered in the wagon.

Chapter Six

"Oh, dear." Polly stood at the front door not knowing what to do. "I'm supposed to go have a talk with Mr. Jones and Ford, but I can't even get into the church."

Bea held up one finger. "Let me investigate." She disappeared into the crowd and, within a few minutes, returned. "Apparently because of the unexpectedly high attendance, Reverend Jones has decided to forgo the pre-ceremony talk. But stay here and I'll be right back. Steve said he'd leave the bridal bouquet with Mrs. Jones."

"I'll wait with you," Fiona Bushnell said to Polly, then turned to her sister-in-law. "You might as well go in and find seats for us."

After Jessica left, the music started.

Polly started to walk up the aisle but Fiona held onto her arm. "Bea hasn't brought your bouquet yet, dear."

"But it's time to go—the music's playing."

"Not yet!" She motioned to John Allsup, the town telegrapher who lived at the Mockingbird Flats Boardinghouse, who'd just come in. "John will escort you up the aisle. No young lady should have to walk alone."

John, a very tall man in his fifties, offered his arm. "I'd be honored, Miss Polly." He still wore his telegrapher's clothes so Polly reckoned he'd likely come to the church straight from work.

"Much obliged."

Bea rushed back with the flowers. "Here you go, Polly. You're a beautiful bride—I so love the daisies with your pink and white dress—you look like a princess. Ford's bound to love what he sees."

Of all people, Bea should know that Ford thought nothing of the sort, nor should he, for as soon as the marriage was annulled, they'd likely never see each other again.

Polly laid her hand on John's arm. "I'm ready." But she wasn't. Her secret wedding would be witnessed by at least forty people. They must have come out of the woodwork to attend her wedding. She

136

didn't see any of the boarders, though, except for John.

She hadn't arranged for the music and she certainly hadn't organized a potluck reception that had been set up outside the church complete with a wedding cake with *Mr. and Mrs. Ford Daily* written on it. She'd go through with the ceremony for the sake of the children, but she had no idea how she'd explain Ford's disappearance after the Children's Society was satisfied that she could legally adopt Noah and Evie.

As she got halfway to the altar, Ford and Steve walked onto the dais from one of the side rooms. Ford had a serious look about him and stood straight as a rolling pin. But once his gaze caught hers, he broke into a grin. That put her at ease some, for she worried he'd be annoyed with her even though she had done nothing wrong—other than agree to marry under false pretenses.

But Ford stood at the altar and waited. His sack suit emphasized his broad shoulders, and his black hair was parted on the side and slicked back. A boutonniere adorned his lapel and he looked all the world like a handsome groom in love with his bride. If only that were true, for she'd always dreamed of a dashing prince sweeping her off her feet. No one knew her private fantasy—Merry didn't even know.

Ladies smiled and gents nodded as Polly passed them. She gripped her bouquet and willed her feet to keep walking. The aisle hadn't seemed so long last Sunday. And all the people! But the one person she most wanted to be there, Merry, was home with the children.

John escorted her to Ford's side, then stepped back once Reverend Jones nodded at him. Then the reverend started talking. Polly made an effort to listen but her palms felt sweaty. Who decided that ladies should wear gloves in the Texas heat? The heavy church air closed in on her but she took short breaths to counteract it.

The reverend got her attention as he said, "...be you well assured, that if you are coupled together for reasons other than God's word allows, then you are not joined together by God, and neither is your matrimony lawful."

Her stomach churned as if a squirrel was chasing a bag of nuts in it and she was grateful when Bea nudged her to offer her hand to Ford.

Reverend Jones nodded at the groom, who took her hand, and that brought her attention back to the reverend's fateful words, or at least his voice. She gazed into Ford's eyes, enchanted with the depth of his character.

In that moment, she knew Ford would always be true and loyal to those he loved. And in the next moment, she felt bereft that she'd never be one of those people. And even though she had only spoken with him twice, she regretted that they'd never get the chance even to get acquainted.

The reverend intoned, "Will you have this woman to be your wedded wife, to live together after God's ordinance in the holy state of matrimony? Will you love her, comfort her, honor, and keep her in sickness and in health, and forsaking all others, so long as you both shall live?"

Ford glanced at Reverend Jones then settled his gaze on Polly, who felt her face grow warm. Just when she thought he wouldn't answer, he said, "I will."

To her, the reverend said, "Will you have this man to be your wedded husband, to live together after God's ordinance in the holy state of matrimony? Will you obey him, and serve him, love, honor, and keep him in sickness and in health, forsaking all others, so long as you both shall live?"

"Reverend Jones," a man called from behind the altar. "I limed the outhouse and cleaned the pot. You want me to start on the windows?"

The townspeople laughed as Reverend Jones turned to his handyman. "You'll have to wait until after the wedding, Yancey. You might as well stay for the reception."

Yancey backed away, his eyes wide. "Damn, uh..." He smacked his hand over his mouth and muttered, "Sorry."

The break gave Polly a chance to convince her voice box to work. When the reverend got back into his position, he said, "Let's continue. Polly?"

"I will." She didn't think it would be so hard to fake a marriage, but she truly believed in these vows and she was committing to a life alone, for she'd never break them.

Once they said their vows to each other, Steve produced a ring and gave it to Ford, who slipped it on her finger. She was so shocked, a tear came to her eye, for she didn't know when he'd had a chance to buy a wedding ring for her.

Reverend Jones cleared his throat to get their attention. "Forasmuch as Manford Daily and Polly Friday Bird have consented together in holy wedlock, and have witnessed the same before God and this company, and thereto have given and pledged their troth either to the other, and have declared the same by giving and receiving of a ring, and by joining of hands; I pronounce that they be—"

Bea let out a shrill scream that could've melted the paint off the walls as she jumped up and down, scattering her bridesmaid bouquet all over the dais and even into the pews, where one petal settled onto Mayor Collins's spectacles. "An earwig—get it off! Get it off!"

Ford grasped Polly by the waist, moved her aside, then flicked the earwig off Bea's arm. "So you're still scared of earwigs?" He laughed.

"Oh, you!" She bopped him over the head with her one remaining flower.

But Polly had a hard time concentrating on the goings-on because her waist still felt the heat of his touch, which nearly took her breath away.

Mr. Jones cleared his throat again. She'd have to make him some lemon tea with honey later. "Are you quite ready to continue?"

Everyone got back to their spots, and Ford guided Polly to hers.

"I now pronounce you man and wife." To Ford, the reverend said, "You may kiss the bride."

Kiss the bride? Polly stifled a gasp. She'd never even given that a thought, but now anticipation mixed with wariness raced through her thoughts. Ford had to be the most kissable man she'd ever met, but it would've been nice to have had some practice before the wedding. On the other hand, a kiss really did seal the vows. Vows taken under false pretenses.

Ford put his hands on her waist and pulled her close enough that she could smell the manly scent of shaving soap—he must've gone to the barber on the way to the florist and the jeweler. He smelled so good—she'd remember that scent until the day she expired.

"Are you ready?" he asked quietly, his low voice settling around her like a warm blanket. "One kiss. That's all it takes."

She took a deep breath and nodded. He leaned in and tilted his head to the left, but she tilted her head to the right so their noses bumped. Then he tilted his head to the right and she went to the left, and their noses bumped again.

"Let's try this another way," he said. He wrapped one arm around her waist and held her chin with the other. "Right on target," he whispered as he lowered his lips to hers.

The second she felt his lips on hers, she thought she'd swoon for sure and she clung to him for strength to keep standing and not to make a fool of herself in front of half the town. But in truth, she wanted to kiss him back, and she wanted it to last a very long time.

"That'll do for now," Reverend Jones said quietly. "Turn toward the congregation, please." When they did, he said in a booming voice, "I present to you Mr. and Mrs. Manford Daily."

The pianist struck up the *Wedding March* again and Ford led Polly down the aisle to the front doors, outside, and then to the reception area on the front lawn, which was mostly dirt but a few brave blades of grass still survived. Fiona swatted at flies and other flying insects that hovered and flitted over the food that was covered in towels—except for the wedding cake, which she protected with vigorous determination.

"Would you like some sweet tea?" she asked. "I sent Dennis to the mercantile in hopes he could find some Champagne or at least some French wine. Of course we'll say a toast to the bride and groom." Her eyes twinkled. "Oh, what fun you'll have tonight."

Jessica came out of the church and made a beeline for Polly and Ford. "I've told my husband—that's Dr. Bushnell—that he'll be seeing you soon."

Polly thought her remark was way beyond indelicate, but Ford just laughed.

"Drumming up business, Mrs. Bushnell?" He grasped Polly's waist and diverted her toward Reverend Jones. "Fewer pests over here," he muttered.

The reverend shook Ford's hand. "Congratulations on your marriage, Mr. Daily, and I'm dreadfully sorry about the interruptions in the ceremony. Yancey donates time every week to do chores around the church and he had a job cancel on him, so he came today. I didn't even think about it when Miss Polly, er, Mrs. Daily made the arrangements. It was just one of those things—my oversight, and I apologize."

"It's all right, sir. You got the job done, and even managed to stay focused when the earwig crawled on Bea's arm."

"I'm still hard of hearing in my right ear." Reverend Jones chuckled. "You and your new missus got off to quite a start. I wish you well and God bless." He craned his neck to look down the table. "I don't suppose Polly brought any of her potato salad."

Chapter Seven

The hot, unforgiving Texas sun bore down on Noah and Evie as they ran as fast as they could from one boulder to the next. Noah didn't know a thing about the country, but he could hide from anyone in the city. He expected he could use the same tactics—just had to find something different to hide behind.

Evie hadn't thrown up a single time so that was lucky, and her shorter legs worked hard to keep up with him, but her hair whipped in the wind as she ran right alongside. The two men who'd given chase threw a couple rocks.

"Scram away from here, you little rascals, and don't come back!" one man yelled.

Evie ducked behind a boulder, leaned over and rested her hands on her skinny knees, and panted. Noah did the same. He wasn't quite as winded as Evie but a little rest wouldn't hurt.

"I don't think they're chasing us anymore," she said once she caught her breath. "Where are we gonna go? Have you thought about that, Noah?"

He shook his head.

"This isn't a town." She swiped at the sweat on her neck. "There ain't a lot of towns out here."

Noah shrugged.

"What are we going to eat?"

He cleared his throat. He'd been practicing at making his voice work without sounding like a rusty hinge, and learning to form words again. He hadn't talked since he'd seen Master Geldart gut a man— that had been at least four years ago. Maybe five. Time passed in a different way on the streets. But if Master Geldart had known Noah could talk, Noah would've met the same fate as the dead man.

"I'm worried, Noah." She straightened and used her hand for a visor as she looked across the Texas landscape. "I don't see nothing but bushes, dirt, and rocks."

He made the sign for pilfering and pointed back to the whiskey wagon.

"Ain't no way I'm going back there," Evie said.

Noah pointed to himself.

"And if they catch you, then what am I gonna do?"

With his fist clenched, he moved it to the side and walked his fingers to follow. Then he made the sign for people at the other end.

"I guess you're right—they'll be driving the wagon to where people are, and it could be a town."

Evie never had any trouble deciphering his gestures—she was the only one who ever understood nearly all he tried to convey. He motioned for her to follow him, which she did.

The harsh sun leeched all the moisture out of his mouth, and he knew Evie was thirsty, too, but she'd die before she'd complain. They needed food, too.

All he could do was hope the wagon got to a town, for he sure didn't want to sleep with rocks and rattlesnakes. The city, he knew. Texas was a whole other matter.

* * *

More people came to the churchyard. Polly estimated close to a hundred, and not just adults—little boys and girls ran around the tables playing tag, squealing and laughing. She missed her own children but knew Merry would take good care of them. Also, the less they knew of the situation, the better. Evie and Noah were only now settling in after a month of being suspicious of her every action, so Polly wanted to make sure neither of them felt as if they were a bother to her.

Ford held her close to his side as befitting a newlywed groom. As the churchyard became more and more crowded, Polly felt more constricted to the point where her feet were telling her to get out.

"Do you think we can leave without causing a fuss?" she asked Ford.

"We've made it through the toast and the cake-cutting, and since we hadn't planned on a party in the first place, we'll go to the instigator, er, Mrs. Bushnell, and let her know we're leaving. Then get the blazes out of here."

He wasted no time maneuvering her through the townsfolk to the cake table where Lavinia Bushnell and Jessica stood, cake servers at the ready.

"Would you like more cake?" Lavinia asked.

"No, ma'am, but it was mighty good."

"Maybe some of Fiona's baked beans, then? They're mighty tasty. She cooks them with ham and onions, then mixes in molasses and a touch of chili."

"Lavinia!" Jessica poked her sister-in-law. "They ought not eat beans on their wedding night, for land's sake."

"We have to be going now," Ford said. "The children have been without their mother all day, and while they're fine with Miss Merry and Mrs. Koch, my bride is getting anxious to see them."

"We understand," Lavinia said.

"We do?" Jessica flinched when Lavinia elbowed her, likely in retribution.

"Everyone line up in two rows," Lavinia called. "We're sending the newlyweds home now."

The townsfolk scrambled to make the lines. Lavinia and Jessica led Polly and Ford to one end. "You just go on through and let everyone give you their blessings."

When she stepped back, Polly whispered to Ford, "I feel like we're running the gauntlet."

"I do believe you're right." He tightened his grasp around her waist. "Let's get this over with."

Polly donned her best smile and walked alongside Ford as folks greeted her. Some tossed beans or wheat, some just said, "Bless your marriage." She thanked them by name and a few insisted on being introduced to Ford, which she did, including to Lavinia's husband Dennis.

"You any relation to Moses Daily?" he asked Ford as they shook hands. "He comes into Mockingbird Flats now and again."

"I'm related to him all right—grandson."

"Thought you looked familiar. You're a chip off the old block, for sure."

"Dennis works at the bank," Polly told Ford. "He and Lavinia also adopted a child from the orphan train."

"Congratulations, Dennis. That youngster is one lucky sprout."

As he spoke, he led Polly away. Leaving the church and all those people was a relief to her, but she didn't begin to feel even remotely comfortable until they finally turned onto the path that led to the boardinghouse.

"I haven't seen the children all day," Polly explained as she picked up the pace. "I hope they didn't miss me too much. Then again, I hope they did—that would mean they're settling in and letting themselves be part of a real family."

"Family's important to you, I expect."

"More important than anything. When you have no family, you understand that in a hurry. Orphans who've been shoved aside or sold often take on the opposite attitude—Merry's boy Calvin has done that, but he'll come around. I think Noah has a dash of that sort of hurt, also. He's mute so that limits what we can communicate."

Ford opened the front door of the boardinghouse for Polly.

Merry greeted them at the door. "I see you've met our new boarder."

"Why yes." She grinned at her sister. "I married him."

"Good, there won't be any impropriety, then. He's staying in the third floor suite across the hall from yours." She shrugged. "Or he was. I guess you two can pick."

"Merry, it's not that kind of marriage. We both have pressing reasons to be married—Ford has to have a wife before his grandfather lets him bring the herd he bought onto the ranch, and now that I'm married, Mr. Ecclestone and the Children's Society will be satisfied. After our business is taken care of, we can get an annulment and go our separate ways."

For some reason, that didn't sound like as good of an idea as it had in Bea's Confectionery that morning. Ford had been courteous as well as generous, not to mention that he was definitely easy on the eyes, and any woman would be proud to have him at her side.

And that kiss—her lips tingled still.

"If you say so." Which meant Merry didn't believe a word she'd said. "I'm helping Elvira serve up supper. You best get your clothes changed. Unless you have other plans, of course."

145

Polly blushed, for she *had* given other plans some brief consideration. "I'll be down to help in a jiffy." Polly glanced around, and not seeing or hearing any children, asked, "Are Noah and Evie playing out back?"

"No. My three are, but yours are up in your suite."

She hurried with Ford and they went up to the third floor. With her hand resting on the doorknob to her suite, she said, "I'll be downstairs if you need anything. Don't be late for supper."

She opened her door and before she knew it Ford had lifted her into his arms as if she were a baby, and she instinctively put her near hand on his back and her other on his shoulder.

"I do believe the tradition is that the groom carries the bride across the threshold."

"We're hardly a traditionally married couple." But she couldn't think of a better place to be than in his arms.

"Even so, I think one kiss is in order."

Before she could object, his lips touched hers, and before she could stop herself, she kissed him right back.

Kissing Ford was certainly not a sacrifice.

Chapter Eight

Ford didn't think it was a good idea to keep kissing her but when she kissed him back, well, he didn't want to stop. Something about Polly drew him like no other woman before. He loved Bea, but more like a sister. The ladies he'd met while attending Cornell were quite pretty but all fluff and giggles. Polly, though, was beautiful, good-hearted, and smart. And irresistible.

When she pulled away, her wide eyes and thoroughly kissed lips gave the impression that she was as dazed as he was. He put her down, and had to steady her when her feet touched the floor.

"Happy wedding day," was the only thing he could think of to say.

She stepped back. "Um, yes. Er..." She glanced about the room, then frowned. "It doesn't look like the children have been in here at all. Not a thing has been moved." She poked her head into a bedroom. "Evie's not in bed."

She rushed to the other bedroom and knocked, but no one answered. She opened the door. "They're gone!"

"Gone? I see they're not here but that doesn't mean they're gone."

"Noah's pillowcase is missing."

Ford didn't know what that had to do with anything.

Before he could ask, Polly rushed out the door and ran down the stairs with her dress hiked up around her knees. "Merry!" She ran down another flight. "Merry, Noah and Evie are gone!"

Ford chased after his new wife-in-name-only. He thought her conclusions were a mite hasty, but her distress was certainly bona fide.

By then the boarders had gathered around the dining room table.

"When was the last time you saw them, Merry?" Polly asked.

"This morning, before I left. Elvira said she'd watch them."

Elvira came out of the kitchen with a big bowl of gravy. "What's that?"

"Did you see Noah and vie after Merry left?"

"Sure did. Evie said she didn't feel well and went upstairs to rest. Noah was with her."

"When was that?"

"Oh, maybe around ten this morning. I hadn't started cooking dinner yet."

Deputy Barnell raised his forefinger. "Miss Polly, er, Mrs. Ford, I saw them just before I was done doing my rounds. They were across the street from the Red Dog. I hollered at them to get on home."

"Why didn't you take them home?"

"On account of I was escorting a prisoner to jail, elsewise I would've."

"I have to go there and see if someone else saw them. Maybe they can tell me where they went."

"Best change clothes first," Ford said. "I'll do the same and saddle my rental horse."

"Saddle my mare, too, just in case." She headed upstairs, unbuttoning as she went.

Ford followed her. "Which horse is yours?"

"The pinto."

"It won't take me as long to change as it will for you. Put something on that you can move around in, for we don't know where this adventure will take us. I'll meet you down at the stable."

Ford went to his room, ripped off the infernal ascot, hooked his sack suit on the wall rather than hanging it in the armoire, and dressed in his riding clothes. It had been a long time since he could wear his comfortably broken-in Texas clothes and they felt danged good. He even buckled on his chaps and strapped on his gunbelt. He was a shade rusty with the pistol but reckoned he could come close to what he was aiming at.

Downstairs, another man sat at the table and Merry called to Ford, "Please come meet Mr. Ecclestone from the Children's Society."

He stopped dead in his tracks, instinctively knowing that this man couldn't be ignored lest Polly lose her youngsters, which was the sum total of the reason why she married him in the first place.

Mr. Ecclestone stood and offered his hand. "Looks as if the

children are safe and sound now that Miss Polly is Mrs. Daily."

"I hope so, for we're happy to be a family. You just hurried things up a mite." Which was stretching the truth, but he couldn't say he was sorry to call Polly his wife. He only hoped she'd come around, and that could take a considerable amount of courting. But first, he had to help her round up the children.

"I brought the adoption papers for you to sign. Your wife has already signed them but she needs to sign again under her married name."

"Glad to." Ford scrawled his signature and dated it. "I'll fetch her if you'll wait a bit—she's dressing for supper."

"Take your time. Looks like the Mockingbird Flats Boardinghouse puts out a fine meal and it would be a pity not to partake at my leisure."

Ford ambled up the first flight of stairs, then took the last two flights two risers at a time and pounded on Polly's door.

"Just a minute," she called.

"No, *now*. I'm coming in." He turned the knob and entered the sitting room. She wasn't there.

"I'm dressing," she said from her bedroom. "I'll be out in a minute."

"It's about your children. A Mr. Ecclestone from the Children's Society is downstairs—you need to sign the adoption papers."

"I already did."

"You need to sign your married name, and you better do it now, before he finds out Noah and Evie are missing. I've already signed. We can use the excuse of going for a buggy ride to get the hades out of here and then we'll head to the Red Dog and see if we can pick up the children's trail."

"Oh, dear." She was quiet for a moment. "Would you come in and help me with the buttons on the back of my dress? I'd have chosen another but this one has a split skirt."

He'd been thinking about her dress—what it hid, more like it. "I'm coming in."

She opened the bedroom door, turned away, then reached back and pulled her hair to the side. There must have been two dozen tiny

149

little buttons. Fastening them all would take some work with his sausage fingers but he'd get the job done. Even though he'd rather unfasten them. But now wasn't the time to be thinking about such things.

"I could do this a lot faster with a button hook," he told her.

"On the dressing table."

He fetched the hook and it worked fine, but he had a hard time not noticing that she didn't wear a corset. Her waist was so small, she sure didn't need one.

"All done. Let's get those papers signed."

"I'll grab my bonnet and gloves."

Downstairs, she greeted Mr. Ecclestone. "I hope you had a good day, and please do take your time and enjoy our supper."

"It's delicious. Compliments to you and your cook."

"If you don't mind, I can sign the papers now. My new husband and I have other plans for the evening and we wouldn't want to be late."

"Of course not." He stood and retrieved the packet from his briefcase. "Sign right next to your husband's name, please."

She did, and handed the papers back to him. "Thank you. We'll be on our way now."

"Congratulations on your marriage. I didn't know you had a beau."

"We haven't known each other very long. You just hurried things up a bit."

"So Mr. Daily said." He sat back down to his meal. "Enjoy your first evening together as man and wife."

Polly waved to everyone as Ford escorted her out of the boardinghouse and to the stable.

"I didn't get a chance to saddle the horses so you wait out front and I'll get it done."

"It'll take half the time if I saddle Lily." She brushed past him, grabbed a curry comb, and headed for her paint mare.

Ford felt awkward letting a lady saddle her own horse, but Polly seemed to know her way around the stable well enough.

And his supposition was right, for she'd saddled her horse just as

150

he was pulling the cinch on his rental.

"If you'll help me up—I have a regular saddle but I ride sidesaddle in town."

He saw the sidesaddle sitting on a sawhorse. "Why didn't you use the sidesaddle?"

"In case we have to do more riding than we hope."

"In that case, we'll have to come back and supply up."

"Saves time from saddling twice."

He couldn't argue with that, and he gladly lifted her onto the saddle—gave him another chance to put his hands on her waist.

They rode straight to the Red Dog Saloon. Cowhands had arrived from surrounding ranches and the party was just getting started. Everyone walked hither and thither except one man who was sprawled on the boardwalk at the side of the saloon.

Polly shifted in her saddle. "Where do we even start?"

"The drunk. Looks like he's been here a while." Ford dismounted. "I'm going to have a talk with him. You stay here, and keep mounted."

"He's passed out."

"I bet if I offer him a drink, he'll wake up in a hurry." Ford went into the Red Dog and after several minutes of waiting in line, came out with a jug of whiskey, which he hid behind his back as he approached the unmoving fellow.

He squatted beside the man, who wore dusty battered clothes, and nudged him. His gray beard was caked and clumpy, and he gripped an empty cup.

"Buddy, have you seen two children in this part of town earlier in the day?"

The man opened one eye. "Might've."

"A boy and a girl?"

"Most likely."

"Which way did they go?"

By now, both of the man's eyes were open but he hadn't moved a muscle. He rolled onto his stomach, pushed himself to his knees then flopped over on his butt in a mostly sitting position that no man could get into if he wasn't three sheets to the wind.

"Don't rightly remember."

"If I fill that cup, will that help your memory any?"

"Could. Let's try it."

Ford poured the cup half full and the man took a drink, some of it spilling out the side of his mouth.

"Now, which way did those children go?"

"Seems like they hid on a whiskey wagon." He took another drink. "Yep, that's sure enough it."

"Which way did the whiskey wagon go?"

The drunk held out his cup. "Might need more memory elixir for that."

Ford filled his cup a little fuller than last time. "I'll give you the rest of the bottle if you tell me everything and tell it true."

"A boy and a younger girl. They hid on the whiskey wagon. That's Duff Doyle's rig."

"You know him?"

"Used to work for him when he traded with the Comanche. He's got a better gig now, selling rotgut in brand name barrels."

"I need to find those children. Which direction did Doyle go? North?"

"North." He grabbed the bottle out of Ford's hand. "Likely to Dailyville, then on to Indian Territory."

"Thanks, buddy. Tell you what, when I get back to town, I'll buy you another bottle. You got a name?"

"Doyle. Sweeney Doyle, Duff's big brother." He took a swig straight from the bottle and went back to sleep.

Ford stood. "Sleep tight, Sweeney."

"We'd better get going while it's still light," Polly said, still horseback.

"First, we need to supply up." Ford took the rental horse's reins from Polly and mounted. He adjusted the reins in his left hand and asked, "Is there a back door to the boardinghouse? Back stairs?"

"There's a door to the kitchen." Polly nudged her mare to a fast walk. "We can go there."

Ford had to urge his horse to keep up with Polly's. "That'll do. Maybe the cook can rustle up a bag of food and some coffee. We can send Merry up to your room to fetch blankets for bedrolls and a change of clothes. I'll ride to the mercantile and hope it's open. We need canteens."

Chapter Nine

"Pull back, Polly," Ford said. "The faster the horses go, the longer they'll need to rest." He pointed to a copse of trees alongside a creek bank. "In fact, we should stop and water the horses up there."

"I know we need to keep a steady pace for the horses' sake. I'm just upset." Polly hadn't been so distraught since Mr. Bird had given her a whipping with a willow switch the day they'd taken her and the three others from the train to the Birds' farm. She'd filched a piece of cake. But she'd been dreadfully hungry and at least had food in her belly when she took the lickin'. "We've been riding for two hours now and haven't found hide nor hair of the children yet."

"They got at least six hours' head start, sugar. Even though wagons go slow, they can cover a lot of territory in six hours. One thing about it, we can be sure they stayed on the road. If they were riding horses, we'd have to track."

"It'll be dark soon. I'm sure they're scared and hungry." The desperation Polly felt resembled that old gut-churning fear that somehow, some way, for whatever reason, she'd been put on this earth by accident, unwanted in any family. As a child, no adult had ever loved her or even been kind to her. She couldn't let that happen with Noah and Evie. They'd had enough hardship already.

"We won't catch up to them before dark—it's almost a certainty. But we do have to take care of the horses and feed ourselves. We might as well overnight here."

"I know you're right about stopping for the night but I'm not feeling very practical right now." And one thing Polly had always been known for was her practicality. Not when it came to her children, though. The sooner she could hug them, the better.

Within a few minutes, they'd arrived at the copse. Ford swung down and the instant his feet hit the dirt, he was already on his way to help her off her mare. As he reached up for her, she braced both hands on his strong shoulders. And even though he held her a mite close on

154

the way down, she couldn't say she minded. In different circumstances, she might've been inclined to hang on a moment longer.

"I'll take care of the horses," he said, stepping back. "You rummage around in the food bag and see what we have for supper."

Polly was all too happy to have something to do. A two-hour horseback ride had given her way too much time to ponder. She preferred not to think about her childhood on the Birds' farm, and she remembered little before then. Noah and Evie were a blessing to her, but more than merely missing them, she felt a responsibility to right the wrongs that had been dumped in their laps for so many of their young years.

She opened the food bag and found a feast. "Ford, do you want cherry pie or peach pie?"

"Both," he called from the stream bank where the horses were drinking. "You pick your favorite and I'll have the other one, for they are both my favorites."

Setting up their supper only took a few minutes so Polly spent the rest of the time chasing off flies, ants, and bugs while watching Ford unsaddle and rub down the horses. He was definitely good scenery and she felt a mite ashamed for appreciating his brawny good looks instead of worrying about Noah and Evie. After all, Merry had called her a champion worrier, *Queen of the Handwringers*.

Something about Ford put a stop to her worries, though, or at least dampened them some. Being around him made her feel as if everything, no matter how dreadful, would be all right. He'd make it that way.

"I'm hungry as a bear," Ford said as he strode toward her. "Want me to make a campfire? I forgot to tell you that I have lucifers in my pocket."

"I'm too hot for coffee, and none of the food needs warmed up, so not having a campfire is one less thing to deal with in the morning."

"Agreed. Let's dig in to our wedding supper."

She served him his plate. He ate everything on it and she did her plate of food justice, too.

He put his fork down and said, "We might as well get to know one another. After all, we're married."

"In name only." But she blushed anyway. Legally, he had every right to claim his husbandly prerogative. And legally, she was obligated to perform her wifely duties. "You go first. I'm not very good at this sort of thing."

"I doubt many of us are," he said. "But I don't mind starting. I grew up on Grandpa's ranch doing all the things that rowdy boys do. My best friend was the segundo's son, Jorge. Of course we could all ride well and I can rope and shoot, brand calves, and all the other chores that need to be done during a roundup. I love the ranch and I never wanted to leave it, but Grandpa Moses decided the Rocking MAD would be more profitable if we didn't have to hire a veterinarian so he sent me to Cornell—that's in Ithaca, New York."

"So you're a veterinarian now?"

"Doctor of Veterinary Medicine, at your service. And a ranchman without a ranch."

"Why on earth did you buy a herd if you didn't have any place to keep the cattle?"

"They'd just come in off the ship from Scotland and the broker was in the saloon crying in his beer that the deal had fallen through. He offered me a heckuva good deal because he didn't want to stay around in the States any longer than he had to. I told the broker that I would buy the whole herd if he would ship them. But later, Grandpa gave me to know that if I hadn't started a family, he wouldn't sign the deed over, and I couldn't buy cattle. Since I already had, that meant I had a herd of purebred Angus cattle and no place to put them."

"Why do you have to have the deed? Couldn't you just rent pasture from your grandpa?"

"He flat out refused, and I know why. It was a transparent ploy to get me to do what he wanted me to do, which was to get married. Now I'm married to a beautiful, smart lady and we'll see what happens when we get there."

She blushed at his compliment but ignored it lest she say something she shouldn't. "Get there?" Polly hadn't planned to go to the ranch at all. "You didn't tell me we were going to the ranch."

"If we don't find the children sooner, we'll be at my home late

156

afternoon tomorrow. It's right along the road so we might as well stop by. Besides, Grandpa Moses might have seen the youngsters and help us out."

"Why is he so dead set on you getting married?"

Ford sighed and rocked back on his elbow. "Grandpa has always lived for family. 'Family first,' he's said a thousand times. But after I left for Cornell, Uncle Junior was killed by a widow-maker, then Grandma passed—Grandpa said of a broken heart."

"And you were gone all this time? That must've been hard for you."

"It was, but it got worse. The next year, my folks came down with yellow fever and he lost both of them. And my three cousins passed from the fever within a few weeks after that. I wanted to come home but Grandpa pointed out that I was better off in Ithaca."

"I'm dreadfully sorry you had to mourn all alone. And to top it, their passings put the Daily legacy squarely on your shoulders." She wondered what it would be like to be part of such a close family, to have a patriarch who really did put family first.

"Yep. Grandpa has two other sons, my uncles, but they headed to the silver mines in Idaho a decade ago and Grandpa Moses doesn't expect they'll ever come back. That leaves me to create the next generation to inherit the ranch."

"So you'll be wanting children from your wife?"

"Of course, but not because of the ranch. Or just because of it. Youngsters are fun to have around and I've always hoped I'd be a father someday—like my pa. I couldn't have asked for a better father. So yes, I do want to have a family. Grandpa's just doing his best to hurry up the process."

* * *

They tidied up the campsite and Ford got out the bedrolls. It was their wedding night but considering the circumstances, he could hardly press the issue of an actual wedding night, although keeping his hands off her was a trial. He had to be content just enjoying her company while quashing his desire to kiss her senseless.

And maybe it was for the best since they'd only met that morning.

He unrolled the blankets. "Where do you want to sleep?"

She lowered her eyes and took a deep breath. "Would you mind terribly if we slept side by side?"

"Not at all. Safety in numbers, they say."

"And, um..."

"Go ahead, Polly. Ask me anything. I'll do whatever I can to make you comfortable. Rocks and stickers don't make for a sound sleep, most generally."

"Would you sleep beside me? It's a new moon and I'm...scared of the dark."

Her raised eyebrows and pursed lips convinced him she was telling the truth about the matter.

"Warmer that way, too." He adjusted his blankets alongside hers.

"I expect so. Texas nights can be cool." But she didn't move a muscle toward her blanket.

He sat on his and toed off his boots, then patted her blanket. "Take your shoes and bonnet off and make yourself to home."

She gazed at him a moment before she sat in a very ladylike fashion.

"Maybe you could tell me a little of your background. I know you were adopted from the orphan train and it didn't work out so well. But what about before that?"

"I lived in an orphanage in New York City."

"And before that?"

"Not much to say. I kept warm and dry when I could and ate when I had food."

The idea of a little girl all alone in the big city made him cringe. How could anyone abandon such a sweet little girl? "How'd you get food?"

"Filched it, or stole money to buy it. Most of the street arabs were accomplished pickpockets and they were happy to teach me."

"Do you remember your folks?"

"No. My only memory is the scent of lavender and a hug. There are a few years where I don't remember anything at all."

"That's a sorry situation—no child should be in such a dire circumstance, yet I know they are, and I regret not paying attention to the urchins begging on the street when I visited New York City."

158

"Not much one man can do. There were thousands of us."

"Which was worse—the orphanage or your adoptive parents' place?"

"The latter. I had such high hopes, and they shattered all my dreams. Merry felt the same. The orphanage was awful—dreary and bleak. They fed us little, and we had to march in line wherever we went. But at least we didn't have false hope."

So that was why Polly was willing to marry a stranger—she didn't want her children to experience the sharp stab of disappointment that she had.

"Did Merry live in the same orphanage?"

"No, we met on the train. Our brothers, too. None of us knew each other before we got on the train."

"Are you planning to marry and have more children?"

"Of course. But when I saw the matron parade the orphan train children through the church and onto the dais, I knew my life wouldn't go according to my girlish fantasy. It doesn't bother me—I learned all about false hope the day I stepped off the orphan train."

"But what if you don't have to give up your fantasy? What if you fell in love?"

"I'd only give in to love if the suitor loved my children and treated them as his own." She slipped between the blankets. "I think we should get an early start."

"I agree, but I have one more question. What if that man were me?"

Chapter Ten

Clanks, creaks, and curses awoke Noah as the whiskey trader and his men hitched up the wagon. Noah and Evie had followed the wagon because he reckoned whiskey wouldn't do the men any good unless they could sell it, and they'd have to go to a town to do it. And that was where he and Evie could find a way to live. Not out in the country—he didn't know a thing about keeping alive in the wilderness.

With a gentle shake, he woke Evie. Once she rubbed the sleep from her eyes, he pointed to the wagon.

"Time to go?" she whispered.

He put his forefinger on his lips to quiet her then nodded.

Neither of them had slept much during the night. He'd tried his best to keep Evie warm and safe, but the rocks had poked his back all night, and some bugs had decided he'd make a good midnight snack. Evie had mostly slept on top of him because she was scared to sleep on the ground, and the howls of the coyotes didn't help.

At least she'd gotten a few hours of sleep and hadn't even thrown up once, but his growling stomach had kept him awake until nearly dawn, and by then he'd been so exhausted, he'd slept despite his misery.

They crept around the boulder and waited while the whiskey trader and his men finished loading the wagon and harnessing the mules. Then, instead of leaving, they all stopped and had a cup of coffee. Noah was anxious to get gone—the sooner they got to a town, the sooner he could filch some food.

Then Evie sneezed. Twice. Three times. The men all looked toward the boulder that he and Evie had hidden behind. Two of them pulled their pistols and shot, likely to scare them off. The bullets ricocheted off the boulder and Noah pulled Evie to the safest spot.

Shots came from the other side and he knew they had to get out of there. He grabbed her hand and took off running, staying behind brush and large rocks whenever he could, but also not losing sight of the road, for they'd be lost forever if he did.

They stayed the course for a long time until the sun was high in the sky. His lips dried up and cracked, and so did Evie's but she didn't complain. He was so thirsty, he even stopped sweating, but they had to go on.

"I can't walk any more, Noah," Evie whimpered. She sagged onto a rock and fanned herself. "New York City... was never... this bad."

He motioned for her to come on.

She shook her head, and after a moment, said, "No, Noah. I'm sorry, but my legs... won't hold me up." She closed her eyes. "You go on... Bring help." She fell to the side and Noah had to jump to catch her head before she bashed it on the rock.

The only thing he could do now was carry her. He picked her up and hoisted her over one shoulder, then staggered back to the road.

* * *

Worry niggled at the back of Polly's mind as her mare plodded along but even so, she couldn't help the odd feeling of excitement, maybe even euphoria, that washed through her every time she glanced at her husband-in-name-only. Ford was dreadfully handsome, but more than that, he was good-hearted and generous.

She'd wakened to the first rays of sun with Ford holding her close. That was a memory she'd cherish to her dying day.

In fact, if it weren't for the boardinghouse she would seriously consider setting her cap for Ford, but Merry couldn't run the boardinghouse by herself and Polly would never, ever abandon her sister. And anyway, could a gal set her cap for a man who was already her husband? It was a strange circumstance.

"Are you faring all right?" Ford asked. "We can stop and rest anytime you want to. Just say the word."

"I'd rather push on. What's the next town we come to?"

"That would be Dailyville."

"I hope we run onto the children before we get there, for it'd be a trial to find them in a city. One thing orphans know is how to hide."

"The only people who live in Dailyville are the folks who work for Grandpa Moses and their families, plus a few merchants and their

161

families. Don't you worry—if our children are in town, we'll find them in no time."

"Our?"

"I signed the papers, too."

"I certainly don't expect you to provide for them so don't burden yourself when it's not necessary. You're just doing me a favor, as I am doing for you."

Ford's gaze was hotter than the noon sun. "Favors don't have to have a time limit."

Polly didn't know what to say back. Since she and Merry had moved to Mockingbird Flats, she'd had several suitors. None of them, nor any of the other men in town, could compare to Ford. The thought had teased her since the moment they'd met at Bea's Confectionery. And if she were honest with herself, she'd have to admit that it was highly unlikely she'd ever meet a man who appealed to her as much as Ford did

They rode another hour before coming up on a nice shady spot beside a creek where they could rest and water the horses. This time, she purposefully waited for Ford to help her down, and when he did, she brushed a kiss across his cheek.

"Mmm, I liked that." He didn't let go of her as he should've. Instead, he pulled her closer and Polly had no inclination to stop him.

"You kissed me at the wedding," she whispered. "I was only returning the courtesy."

"Sugar, what I feel for you right now has nothing to do with courtesy." He kissed her so deeply she thought she float right off the ground. Then he set her away from him. "Any more of that, and I'll never get the horses tended."

She cleared her throat. "I'll, uh, fill the canteens."

* * *

Noah dreamed he was floating in a nice soft cocoon with cool water bathing his face. He didn't want to open his eyes and spoil it all, but he had enough wherewithal to know he needed to check on Evie. When he did open his eyes, lace curtains wafted in the breeze over him, and his cocoon was a feather bed.

An old man with kind eyes and a scraggly beard dabbed at Noah's

162

face with a wet cloth. "Good to see you're finally awake. Looks like you and your little sister got a little overheated out there. You was in quite a pickle when we run onto you sprawled out on the road."

His sister? Noah had to know if Evie was all right and tried to gesture the question, but the old man didn't catch it.

"She's quite a talker. Says you don't talk at all, though. Is that right?"

Noah nodded.

"Don't you go worrying none about her. She's downstairs with Margaret—she's my cook—mixing up a double batch of oatmeal cookies. By the smell, I expect you can sample some in a few minutes."

Noah was relieved to hear that, and he sure did like cookies, but wondered what he should do—get Evie out? But he was so tired. The old man seemed nice enough. That could change as quick as a gust of wind, though.

People were nice until they didn't get what they wanted from you. Noah had learned that over and over again. Except Mama Polly, and Aunt Merry—after a month, he'd decided they were genuinely kind ladies.

"I'll even keep it a secret that you can talk," the old man said. "Even Evie doesn't need to know if you don't want her to."

Noah sat up like a shot and stared at the old man.

"By the way, I'm Moses Daily. You can call me Grandpa Moses if you want." He swished the cloth around in a bowl of water, wrung it out then handed it to Noah. "You better keep this on your face. You got yourself quite a sunburn, and I expect your skin will peel as it is. The cooler you keep it, the less it'll hurt tomorrow. Maybe Margaret has some pickle juice to put on it."

He leaned back in his chair. "I also expect you want to know how I know you can talk."

Noah nodded.

"That's on account of you jabbered like a magpie the whole while you was passed out and feverish. You didn't stop talking until your fever broke a little bit ago. If you want to know what you said, I took a few notes."

He tapped his noggin. "The memory ain't as good as it used to be."

Noah hadn't talked for so long, he didn't remember how to answer questions that weren't questions, but he sure did want to know what he'd said.

"Let me tell you about my big brother." Grandpa Moses pointed a picture on the wall. It was of a young man dressed in a suit. "He got in the way of a bunch of Indians. They was likely on a hunting party or some such and didn't have time for prisoners or entertainment so they let him go. But before they did, they told him if he so much as said one word, they'd cut his tongue out. So he didn't say a word. He got back home all right, but he didn't talk for more than a year."

The old man stood and flexed his back. "Danged rheumatism." He tousled Noah's hair. "When you want to have a little chat, come on downstairs. We have lots of food, too, if you feel up to having a meal. Looks like you and your sister could use a little meat on your bones."

He handed Noah a peppermint stick. "This might settle your stomach some. I'll fetch you some tea and bring another pitcher of water. There's a chamber pot under the bed."

Noah really wanted to say something to the old man who'd offered for a strange boy to call him grandpa but he couldn't think of a single clever thing. He swallowed and took a breath.

"Thanks, Grandpa Moses."

Chapter Eleven

Ford had mixed feelings. He hadn't seen his home in six years and he'd missed it sorely every single day.

"We'll be at the ranch soon," he told Polly. "This is where we played when I was a boy. Those rocks over there make a great fort."

"What if my children aren't there?"

"I don't know where they could've gone other than the ranch— maybe Dailyville, but I doubt it."

He and Polly had run across the whiskey wagon that morning. It was stopped for a busted wheel. When Ford asked the whiskey trader if he'd seen a boy and a girl, he'd said, "Yep. They was stowed in our wagon. I ran 'em off last night but they snuck around—stole some cooked rabbit, too—so my men ran them off for good this morning."

"How far back was that?"

"Oh, about a mile, I expect."

Polly had been appalled. "You abandoned those children in the middle of nowhere?"

"Hell, they ain't mine. Their folks ought to keep a better eye on them."

Ford and Polly had ridden three hours since then.

"The ranch house is up ahead just around the bend. If Noah and Evie aren't there, Dailyville is just a couple miles beyond. I'm almost positive we'll find them, and if we don't, we'll round up a search party. We'll have the children back to you by nightfall."

She'd been quiet the last few miles. She brushed the dust off her face and then said, "I surely hope so." Then after a bit, she added, "Will your grandfather be at the ranch house?"

"Most likely. I guess we'll find out."

A quarter of an hour later, they rode into the barnyard. A big happy dog greeted them with excited barking and a vigorously wagging tail.

"Well, here we are—the Rocking MAD, best ranch in all of

Texas."

He dismounted and looped the reins around the hitching post, then helped Polly off her mare.

By then, a stablehand Ford didn't recognize trotted out from the barn. "I'll take good care of your horses during your visit, sir."

"Much obliged." Ford guided Polly onto the big wraparound porch. "I don't know whether to knock on the door or not. It's my own house so there's no need to knock, right? But they don't know I'm here, so I don't wanna surprise anyone."

"I just want to know if my children are here." She licked her lips—the lips he wished he could kiss right then. "And I wouldn't mind a tall glass of water."

Ford decided to do both. First he knocked then he opened the door. "Margaret, are you here?"

She trotted her hefty self to the door, gasped, and flung her arms around him. "Well if it ain't our Ford!"

She squeezed his cheeks between the palms of her hands. "You're just as handsome as your grandpa if I do say so myself."

He chuckled, then stepped back and put his arm around Polly's waist. "Margaret, meet my wife, Polly."

Margaret eyed his bride up and down. "My stars, you sure did find yourself a pretty one."

Polly curtsied. "Thank you, ma'am."

"You must be hungry and thirsty." The cook crooked her index finger. "Come into the parlor. We don't put on airs here, so just make yourself comfortable. I'll go fetch Moses. There won't be a happier man on the face of this earth when he sees the two of you. Then I'll rustle up some food for you."

After she went upstairs, Ford remembered that Polly's lips were dry from thirst—he didn't want to wait for the cook to fetch a glass of water when he could get it himself. "I'll be right back with your drink." He sniffed and smiled. "And maybe some of Margaret's famous oatmeal cookies."

When he walked into the kitchen, he couldn't have been more surprised. A little girl was scooping cookies onto a platter.

"Those cookies look mighty fine, miss, and they smell even better.

166

Would you mind putting a few on a saucer for me and my wife?"

The girl's arms were so scrawny, they looked like sticks with skin pulled over them. "Did Grandma Margaret say you could have some?"

"Not exactly, but I bet she wouldn't mind, and we're both hungry." He pumped a glass of water. He didn't know Margaret had had children, let alone grandchildren. "I'm Ford. Moses Daily is my grandpa. What's your name?"

"Evelyn, but I go by Evie. And Grandma Margaret isn't really my grandma, but she said to call her that."

"Evie?" She must be Polly's adopted daughter. "What's your last name, Evie?"

"I don't rightly know anymore. I guess it would be Evie Bird." She put the last cookie on the plate and handed it to Ford.

"Tell you what, come with me. I have a surprise for you."

"Is it sweet?" She followed him down the hall.

"Sweetest I ever saw."

When they got to the parlor, Evie came to a dead stop. "Mama Polly!"

Polly sprang from the couch and practically smothered the little girl with hugs. "I was so worried about you and Noah."

"I missed you, 'specially last night. It was scary. And we got really hungry. I don't like sleeping on the ground."

"Where's your brother?" Polly was teary-eyed so Ford gave her his handkerchief.

"Upstairs. He tried too hard to take care of me and he fell and he didn't get up. I thought he was dead for sure, but then I was so tired, I fell asleep right there on the road. Then an old man came along and said he'd give us food and a place to sleep. He picked up Noah and put him in the back of the wagon on some straw. I stayed with Noah and tried to get him to drink from the canteen but he wouldn't."

"My stars, that sounds harrowing. Are you all right? How's your stomach?"

"I didn't puke once while we were gone." Evie beamed a smile, then frowned then heaved all over Polly and the parlor rug.

"I'll get a bucket of water and a rag," Ford said as he took off for

167

the kitchen.

By the time he got back, Grandpa Moses was standing in the parlor doorway and Margaret was fussing over Polly.

"Welcome home, Ford. Margaret said you brought your bride. She don't look old enough to have a girl Evie's age."

He held up the bucket. "Uh, I have to get this to Polly. Evie got sick."

"I see that." Grandpa Moses stepped back. "Is the boy hers, too?"

"Yes," Polly said. "He's mine. Is he all right?" She wiped her neck and dabbed at her bodice.

"He's fine. But looks like your husband ought to pick you up and carry you to the horse trough. He can shuck you down and throw water on you. It'd be a whole lot faster, and Margaret could get to the rug faster, too. I'll help her take it up."

"I'm sorry!" Evie wailed. "I didn't puke or poop one single time while we were running away."

Polly wiped Evie's mouth with a clean cloth. "Never you mind—we'll get this cleaned up. You're not in trouble. And you're safe."

After Ford thought about it a minute, he decided his grandpa was right. "Stand up, Polly, and I'll carry you outside. Then I'll come back in and get Evie. Grandpa and Margaret can take care of the parlor. We'll have everything cleaned up in a lamb's shake."

"And I'll bring one of Ford's mother's dresses for you to put on," Margaret said. "Moses, help me move the couch and the end table so we can take up the rug."

Ford helped Polly stand then he put one arm behind her knees and lifted her like a baby. "Let's go, sugar."

"But you're getting yourself all messy."

"I'm a veterinarian—we get messy. It all cleans up."

By then he'd carried her outside and set her down by the trough. "Need help getting those clothes off?" He didn't know whether he was being helpful or had succumbed to wishful thinking. Maybe a little of both. Vomit did put a damper on things, though.

"Let's just get this over with." She worked at the buttons on the back of her dress and cursed every one of them. "Could you give me a hand with these buttons again?"

"No button hook. Tell you what, how about I cut your dress off?"

She hid her face in her hands. "This is so embarrassing."

"I'm your husband—we can't explain to Grandpa that you're embarrassed."

"Just get the thing off and go fetch Evie so I can clean her up, too." She sounded a mite cross.

Ford took out his knife and sliced the buttons off carefully so as not to harm the material, and he even managed to retrieve most of the buttons and stash them in his pocket. As he finished the last one and pushed the dress off her shoulders, he heard a rumble.

He glanced down the road and saw a big cloud of dust. "Must be a sandstorm coming." He grabbed a bucket, dipped it in the trough, and doused her. "We best get you in the house. We can clean up Evie in the mud room."

But it wasn't a sandstorm—before he could pick up her dress, they were surrounded by black Angus. Big, snorting, stomping cows.

Polly screamed.

* * *

Polly couldn't move on account of the fear that seized her. Nor could she utter a peep, for her throat tightened and memories of nearly being stomped to death in a stampede on the Birds' farm overtook any good sense she had left. Hooves kicking her back, clods in her teeth and eyes. Her brothers had saved her but took a thrashing for not staying with the herd.

"I thought you were a farm girl." Ford waved his arms to shoo the Angus away from Polly.

She sidled closer to him. But her legs weren't working any better than her throat and all she could do was hang onto his arm. His strength was her only comfort and she couldn't let go.

"Run to the house, sugar, not to me. I'll herd them into the corral."

All she could do was shake her head and cling to him.

"All right, I'll take you there." Ford tossed her over his shoulder and headed for the porch. He climbed the two stairs and deposited her in his grandpa's rocking chair. "Stay up here. The cattle won't come

169

up the steps unless they're spooked, which they won't be if you don't scream again."

He bent and gazed into her eyes. "You've got to calm down, sugar. Take a couple deep breaths for me."

She did so then worked up all her strength to give him half a nod. But when he left, all she could focus on was the milling black cows in the cloud of dust.

Noah busted out the door and stood between her and the cows, waving his arms just like Ford had done. A calf bounded up beside his mother and it looked like he was going to join them on the porch, but Noah yelled, "Heeyah!" The calf scampered back to his mama.

Noah's yell snapped Polly back into reality. He'd talked! Well, almost. Yelled, anyway. She stood and wrapped her son in a big bear hug. "Oh, Noah, you yelled at that calf! I'm so happy." She hugged him again.

"You're squeezing the stuffin' outta me," he croaked.

"Could you all along?"

He nodded as he gasped for air.

"I'm so happy for you." She hugged him tighter. "I hate to think what caused you to have to use the no-talking tactic, but I'm so happy you don't need it now."

Evie bounded onto the porch and piled into the hug. "You can talk, Noah. You can talk! I knew you could."

Polly choked back a sob. Even though the cows were still way too near for her comfort, Noah's words meant he had a brighter future ahead, and no parent could ask for any more than that.

"Mama Polly," Evie said, "Noah's face is turning blue. Maybe you should give him some air."

Polly did ease up but she didn't let go. Noah and Evie had wormed their way into her heart, and while she hadn't birthed them, she loved them just the same.

"Well, Noah," Grandpa Moses said as he walked onto the porch. "You done let the cat out of the bag." He chuckled. "Daughter, you look like a drowned rat."

That was when Polly realized she'd displayed herself in front of everyone in only her chemise. She huddled down and crossed her

A FAMILY FOR POLLY

arms over her breasts. "Oh, dear!"

Margaret hurried to her with a dressing robe. "This was Ford's mama's robe. You can have it." She crooked her finger at Evie. "You come with me, young lady. We'll get you bathed and changed."

Polly wrapped herself in the robe then peered through the dust to see if she could find Ford. He seemed to know exactly what to do so she wasn't worried, but she sure felt relieved when she spotted him. He had the gate open and one batch of cattle bunched, but he couldn't bunch them and drive them in at the same time.

Grandpa Moses patted Noah on the shoulder. "I brung you a glass of water. Drink it then we'll help your pa gather those cows." While Noah downed the water in about three gulps, Grandpa said to Polly, "You best get on in the house. Looks as if you could use a nap. We men..." he tousled Noah's hair "...will take care of things out here."

Noah looked so proud—he puffed up his chest and pursed his lips. "Let's get to it, Grandpa."

Then he fainted.

Chapter Twelve

By the time Ford got the cattle settled, it was time for supper. He looked forward to sitting down to one of Margaret's fine meals, and she'd outdone herself with freshly baked bread, beef stew, and pecan pie.

"No one can make pecan pie like Margaret," he said as he sat beside Polly. "Don't fill up, for you'll surely want a second piece of pie."

"Oh, you." Margaret gave him a full bowl of stew. "Always wanting dessert first. But mind you, eat all your stew."

"I could eat a whole tub of it right about now. Pickin's were slim on the trail." He scanned the room. "Where're Noah and Evie?"

"Both tucked safely in bed," Polly said. "I think we should call a doctor."

"I'll check on them—animal doctor, sure, but people have blood and skin and bones, too."

"I'd appreciate it greatly."

"Mostly likely, Noah's dehydrated both from lack of water and his sunburn. We'll have to keep him inside for a few days and pour the water to him, both inside and out. Then, when we let him go out, we need to make sure he wears long sleeves and a wide-brimmed hat."

"I'm going into town tomorrow," Grandpa said. "I'll buy him one."

"Thanks," Polly said.

"By the way," Ford said, "I sent a message with the drover to take to Dailyville. Everett—that's the telegrapher—will have wired your sister by now, so she knows where you and the children are."

"That was very kind of you."

"Eat your supper." Margaret passed the bread. "If you can't talk and eat, don't talk."

Ford laughed, but he ate a spoonful of stew and then took a slice of bread. "You don't know how much I missed hearing that." He used his fork to point at the butter beside her. "Are you hoarding the butter these days?"

She laughed and passed it to him.

When time came for dessert, Ford waited for Polly to sample the pie.

"Mmm, you're right, Ford. This is the best pecan pie I've ever tasted." She turned to Margaret. "Would you mind sharing your recipe?"

"I don't have one, but I'll be glad to show you how I make it and you can take notes."

"Oh, but we'll be needing to leave soon. My sister can't possibly run the boardinghouse by herself."

Ford finished off his pie than sat back and rubbed his belly. "Those children aren't going anywhere for a while. They need to regain their strength."

He never thought he'd be grateful for sick youngsters, but they'd buy him a few days to convince Polly to stay with him. He'd have to work fast, though, and it took time to earn a skittish filly's trust.

"You're right, but I hate to impose."

Grandpa Moses leaned forward in his chair. "Young lady, there's no such thing as imposing on your family. We take care of our own."

"I dusted your parents' room," Margaret said to Ford. "It's a bigger room than yours and has a full bed, so it makes sense for you to sleep there. I put Noah in your old room, and Evie wanted to stay in my room. When she gets more comfortable, she can move to the room by Noah's."

* * *

After dawdling as long as she could, Polly finally followed Ford upstairs to the bedroom. She wanted nothing more than to be alone with him, yet nothing scared her more, for she was in jeopardy of falling in love with this man—and his family, too.

He opened the door and she entered ahead of him.

"I love the wallpaper." It was off-white with small blue flowers in columns with narrow blue scrollwork lines in between.

"Ma liked it." Ford took off his vest and hung it on a hook beside the armoire that matched the bedframe and the nightstands. "Pa put up with it. He painted everything white, but if Ma wanted something, he'd make sure she had it."

Polly chattered on a bit, knowing she used small talk to delay what need to be discussed. But finally, she said, "I'll make a bed on the floor for the night."

"Not a good idea," Ford said. "There's not much Margaret doesn't notice, and she'd figure out right off that we hadn't slept together. Besides, we slept together last night."

They had, and Polly loved lying by his side, sharing his warmth. She'd felt so safe. But it wasn't right to let him think they could engage in normal marital duties when they planned on getting an annulment.

"All right, if you sleep on top of the covers and keep your longjohns on."

"That'll be a might hot, but you have a deal." He toed off his boots and then took off his shirt. "Need me to help you with your corset?"

"No..." Her voice trailed off because she didn't want to admit that she hadn't even brought one. "But I sure wouldn't mind a bath."

"We have a washroom downstairs and hot water in the stove reservoir. I'll draw you a bath, and when you're done, I'll hop in." He opened the armoire where a few ladies' garments were hanging. "You can have any of Ma's clothes that you want to tide you over until we can buy you some from town. Margaret said there are underthings in the drawer."

After their baths and they were back in the room, the time came to blow out the lantern and get to bed. She looked forward to sleeping with him but she also knew she was in dangerous territory. She could very well end up back in Mockingbird Flats with a broken heart, while he lived happily ever after with his wonderful family and a lucky woman for a wife.

She crawled under the covers and yawned. "It's been a long day." And it would be a longer night.

Ford lay beside her. "You can use my shoulder for a pillow. Don't worry, I won't take liberties."

Polly was tempted to entice him, for then she had a chance to keep him as her husband, but she could never do such a thing. First and foremost, she wanted a husband who loved her. She'd give anything if that were Ford.

* * *

The children flourished at the Rocking MAD the following week and Polly loved seeing them so happy. Merry had wired back that there was no need to hurry home, so Polly let Noah and Evie have their fun.

Ford had given them ponies, and while Evie enjoyed riding, Noah loved his pony and was turning into quite the rider.

"Look, Ma, I can do a trick!" Noah kicked his pony to a trot, then looped the reins around the pommel and held up both hands. He stayed rock solid in the saddle.

"That's wonderful, Noah. You sit an excellent seat—good balance."

"Pa says I'll make a good cowhand in no time. He's showing me how to rope."

Since when did they start thinking of Ford as their father? Since the day they got here, that's when.

Ford came up behind her and put both hands around her waist. "He's doing good for a city boy. In another month, you won't be able to tell he wasn't born in Texas."

"We won't be here another month."

"I hope you reconsider. I think we make a fine family."

"You want me to stay?"

"More than anything."

She wanted to stay, and even more than that, she wanted him to love her, for she'd lost her heart to him. "Merry can't run the boardinghouse by herself. Elvira helps with the cooking, but then we have to change the sheets once a week and there's a lot of cleaning to do, not to mention yardwork, plus I do all the bookkeeping. We can barely keep up as it is with the two of us."

"Do the children want to go back?"

"You know the answer to that."

Evie flitted around the springhouse like a happy little sparrow as she romped with the dog. She wore a wide smile and she was actually

175

gaining weight. Ford had put her on a diet of all meat and vegetables. His thinking was that since she didn't get sick when they'd run away, and she'd only eaten a little rabbit then, that they ought to try eliminating grains for a while. It was a successful experiment and while Evie looked longingly at the cakes and cookies, neither did she want to get sick, so she'd kept to the diet without Polly fussing at her.

Polly turned to Ford, his hands still on her waist. "I hate to go. I don't want to leave the ranch any more than the children do, and I've grown very fond of Grandpa Moses and Margaret, too, but..."

"But what?"

"The longer I stay, the harder it will be to leave."

"Then don't go. Be my wife for real. I want you to stay with me, and I want to be a real father to Noah and Evie." He pulled her close. "And a real husband to you." He kissed her, at first sweet and tender, then deeper with passion.

The whole world melted away—all her troubles and concerns. Just his kiss. She knew it for sure—she wanted a lot more than a kiss. She held him dear.

"Ahem." Grandpa came up behind them and chuckled. "I know Noah's gonna need some help with the ranch in ten years, but you can work on getting a little brother for him after supper."

Polly blushed as she stepped away from Ford. "We were, uh, discussing my return to Mockingbird Flats."

"I see that. This old goat knows a mite more than you think I do." He handed the signed deed to Ford. "Evie said she'd never seen Ford until you two came to the ranch, and earlier, Noah said he heard a man tell you that if you didn't get married, he'd take Noah and Evie back and put them on the orphan train again. And Ford knew dang well it was past time for him to start a family. I had to push the matter a mite."

She didn't say a word and Ford ran his hand down the side of the envelope without looking at it.

"Yep, I'm right." Grandpa ran his hand through his beard. "I never seen two people try to act like they was in love in front of others, then acting like they wasn't in love to each other, when the only ones who didn't know they was in love was them. But you'll figure it out."

176

He clapped Ford on the shoulder. "Go ahead and take her back if she wants to go. You might ask the young'uns whether they want to stay or go first, though. You're their father in the eyes of the law and in their eyes, too."

Polly gasped. "I couldn't possibly leave my children!"

"Now in that matter, you have to do what you think is best for them, and that's all I'm gonna say. Proceed with your good-bye kiss."

Chapter Thirteen

After supper, Grandpa Moses got up. "Who wants to listen to a little music?"

"I do," the children chorused.

"You up to playing a few tunes?" he asked Margaret. "I'll help with the dishes."

"She's not washing them," Polly said. "I am. She's put in a long day."

Ford stood and started stacking plates. "Then I'll help. We'll make quick work of it."

"I'll dry," Evie said. "And Noah can feed the dog."

Within twenty minutes, they'd completed all the nightly chores and were seated in the parlor, each with a tall glass of sarsaparilla. Margaret took her place at the piano and struck up a sentimental favorite, *My Old Kentucky Home.*

"Are you originally from Kentucky?" Polly asked Margaret.

"Nope. Born and raised in Fort Worth. Came to the Rocking MAD with my husband, and been here ever since." She flipped the pages in her songbook and said, "How about *When Dear Friends Are Gone?*" then struck up the chords before anyone could answer.

"Let's have a little dance music," Grandpa suggested. He stood and offered his hand to Evie. "Miss Evie, may I have the next dance?"

Polly followed his lead and asked Noah to partner with her. What a joy it was to be part of a family that enjoyed each other's company. She'd dreamed of this.

"I don't know how to dance." Noah stayed in his chair so Polly pulled him to his feet.

"There's only one way to learn."

Midway through the song, Ford cut in on his grandpa and danced with Evie who'd caught on to the steps by standing on Grandpa's boots. Noah watched and soon he'd caught on, too.

After the song ended, Grandpa motioned for the children to come with him. "Margaret will keep playing so you'll have music to sleep by." He turned to Polly. "Don't you worry yourself—I've put young'uns to bed before and none of them kicked the bucket."

Margaret smiled softly and began playing *Annie My Own Love*.

Ford pulled Polly into his arms and whispered, "I think of this song as *Polly My Own Love*."

They swayed to the music and Polly's heart was filled with love. She smiled at him and he brushed a kiss across her lips. "Stay with me always, Mrs. Daily."

"But Merry—"

"We'll visit every couple of weeks if you want. I'll hire a maid and a bookkeeper. If your sister is half as resourceful as you are, she'll be fine."

Polly wanted to believe him.

"Be my wife, Polly. I truly do love you and my heart's desire is that we'll be together for the rest of our days. I'll be a good husband and a good father to our children. Will you stay?"

Polly clutched him and stopped dancing. "I liked you the moment we met at Bea's Confectionery. I trusted you when Bea thought our marriage of convenience was a good idea. She'd never have gone along with it if you weren't a good man. And I've loved you since the moment I saw you in the church. You clinched it when you saved Bea from the earwig. But what really made me realize you were the man for me was when you went out of your way to help me find the children—and then teaching Noah how to ride and rope."

"Is that a yes?"

She smiled at him. "That's a yes."

Margaret put the cover down on the piano. "My day is done. Good night, love birds."

"Let's go to our room," Ford said. "We have some catching up to do in our marital duties."

Polly grabbed her sarsaparilla. "Just in case we get thirsty."

Epilogue

Two years and fifty-one weeks later

Even though Ford made sure Polly and the children visited Mockingbird Flats often, she was tickled when he turned the wagon up the lane to the boardinghouse, for she missed her sister dreadfully.

Ford called Noah, who clambered over his sisters and the luggage to get to the back of the driver's seat. "Think you can run in and get Calvin and Blake to help unload?"

"Sure thing."

Ford scowled at his wife. "I do believe we've brought half our household belongings."

She scowled right back, but knew they were both teasing. "You name one thing we won't need."

He blew out his cheeks. "I give."

Noah laughed. "Aunt Merry will think we're moving back in."

"They'd have to build on again," Ford said. "The third-floor suite won't hold us any longer now that you and Evie have a little sister and a baby brother."

"I still think it's silly to call a baby *Manny*. He ain't a man." Noah hopped off the wagon before it stopped and was running before his feet hit the ground. "Calvin!"

His cousin ran out to meet him and they clapped each other on the shoulder in the grown-up way that older boys do. Polly wanted to get out of the wagon, too, but with a nursing baby in her arms and a toddler ready to break for freedom, she had to be content to wait until Ford helped her down.

"I'm so excited for the party!" Evie, who'd gained enough weight to look hale and hearty, straightened her little sister Stephanie's dress and kissed her chubby cheek. "We get to see our cousins!"

Evie had worked for months making all kinds of crafted items for her cousin Abigail and her new twin cousins, who were within a month the same age as Stephanie. "How come Stephanie and Manny

180

don't get presents?"

"Because we know when their birthdays are," Polly answered. "But we don't know the dates of birth for you, Noah, Calvin, Abigail, and Tammie, so we have an adoption day party instead."

"I think we have the better deal," Evie said. "Because we're having a big party. The biggest!"

By then, Ford set the brake, chocked the wheels, and had done all the fiddling he needed to do. He held out his arms to the girls. "Let's get the princesses off the wagon." He took one in each arm and set them on the ground. "Evie, better make sure your little sister doesn't dash under the horses' hooves while I'm getting your mama and brother down."

"Polly!" Merry hurried out of the boardinghouse and hugged her sister and baby nephew. "Everyone's here and the table's set." She kissed her sister on the cheek again.

Blake finally caught up to his wife. "Ford, I'll unhitch the team. You better get your tribe settled."

"You're just shirking twins duty."

"Sharp man."

Merry poked his ribs. "You know they're fine with Elvira and Abigail." She turned to Polly and took the baby. "He's so sweet! Just wait a year."

Polly rescued Stephanie, who was halfway across the yard studying a weed in full seed. "Evie, you can go in the house and play with Abigail now. I'll take care of your sister."

Evie tugged on her box of goodies. "I'm taking my presents in first."

Noah and Calvin ran to the wagon.

"I'll take it," Calvin said as he hefted the box over his shoulder. Noah grabbed the baby's bag and a valise, and the two of them headed for the boardinghouse.

"How did Noah and Evie do in school this year?" Merry asked Polly after all the children had left.

"Very well. This last year, Noah went from fourth grade to sixth—a grade ahead. Evie's spot on and she'll be in fourth grade next year. Of course, Stephanie wants to go to school with them but she'll have to wait her turn. And yours?"

"They've done well, too, despite the distraction from the twins.
Calvin's very bright and Abigail keeps right up with him."

The suite Polly had thought so spacious when she'd first moved
Evie and Noah to the third floor now seemed small. She took baby
Manny from Ford and put him in the bassinet. "It's amazing how the
smallest humans take the most space."

Ford took his wife in his arms. "Doesn't matter, as long as we
always share whatever space is left over." He laid a toe-curling kiss
on Polly and she clutched his strong shoulders ready for more.

"Ahem." Noah stood in the doorway. "We're lighting the candles
now.

Polly grabbed the baby and they all headed down to the dining
room. John Allsup, Bass Barnell, and Gideon Warren met them and
congratulated them on their new arrival.

"We fellows will have a cigar later," John offered, patting his vest
pocket. "And maybe a wee dram of brandy."

Polly noticed Bass had a lady friend with him. Since he'd never
once brought a lady to the boardinghouse, she was very curious about
her. Polly smiled at her and said, "I'm Polly Daily. And you?"

Bass pulled her to his side. "This here's my wife, Neva Jo."

"Your wife?" Polly had never known him to even court a woman,
and Merry hadn't mentioned it, either.

"We've been married for eight years." Neva Jo gazed up at her
husband. "I was too young—not in years, but of a mind. I finally
realized a woman can't get any better husband than what I already
had."

Elvira banged the gong. "Let's get the party started!"

The children had a great time. After they'd eaten their fill of cake
and cookies, Merry ushered them into the back yard to play while the
adults recovered. Meantime, Polly and Merry stole a little sister time
to catch up.

Later that night, when Polly and Ford finally got the children
settled down and in bed, Polly snuggled up to Ford's side.

"Remember that nasty Mr. Ecclestone?"

"Sure do. He's a hard man to forget."

"I'm thankful to him every single day, because if he hadn't been so unreasonable, I'd never have proposed to you."

"I hadn't thought of it that way." Ford kissed her on the nose. "Speaking of which, I owe you one."

"You do?"

"Yes." He braced himself over her. "Will you be my wife forever?"

"Ford Daily, you've made me the happiest woman in the world. I will."

About Jacquie Rogers

Jacquie is a former software designer, campaign manager, photographer, deli clerk, and cow-milker. She was a Golden Heart Finalist. Her 2007 release, *Faery Special Romances*, won the Fall NOR Award for Best Print Sci-fi/Fantasy Romance. She has donated all royalties from this collection to the Children's Tumor Foundation, helping to end neurofibromatosis through research. She has contributed to several anthologies and series.

In addition to numerous other awards, her Hearts of Owyhee Series has won acclaim as well as a Laramie Award Grand Prize. Her first two Honey Beaulieu novels, *Hot Work In Fry Pan Gulch* and *Sidetracked In Silver City*, won four Will Rogers Gold Medallion Awards in 2017. Jacquie teaches several workshops both online and in person.

Find Jacquie on the Net:

Website http://www.jacquierogers.com

Blogs: http://jacquierogers.blogspot.com/

Facebook: http://Facebook.com/groups/JacquieRogers/ (her Facebook group)

https://www.facebook.com/JacquieRogersAuthor/

Twitter: https://twitter.com/jacquierogers